TO SERVE TWO MASTERS

There was an area set aside for the display of slaves: an enclosed yard where men were discussed, priced and sometimes even exchanged.

We stood obediently, the three of us in a row. Master sat on a wooden bench and waited for one of the traders to show interest.

Justin was the first to be examined. The man who approached him was half-naked. He was hairy and coarse, but obviously a wealthy freeman of some sort. He squeezed Justin's pink, round nipples slowly and thoughtfully.

Justin's nipples are very sensitive and the pressure made him squirm slightly. Like the other two of us, he had been anchored by the chained collar around his neck to a nearby post. He strained on his lead. This seemed to please the man and he patted Justin's curly, golden hair. He then asked our Master some questions. Master replied by making Justin bend over at the waist and inviting the man to put his finger into the waiting arsehole. We had all learnt to get well used to such invasions.

TO SERVE
TWO MASTERS

Gordon Neale

First published in Great Britain in 1998 by
Idol
an imprint of Virgin Publishing Ltd
332 Ladbroke Grove
London W10 5AH

ISBN 0 352 33245 X

Cover photograph by Colin Clarke Photography

Typeset by SetSystems Ltd, Saffron Walden, Essex
Printed and bound in Great Britain by
Cox & Wyman Ltd, Reading, Berks

SAFER SEX GUIDELINES

These books are sexual fantasies – in real life, everyone needs to think about safe sex.

While there have been major advances in the drug treatments for people with HIV and AIDS, there is still no cure for AIDS or a vaccine against HIV. Safe sex is still the only way of being sure of avoiding HIV sexually.

HIV can only be transmitted through blood, come and vaginal fluids (but no other body fluids) – passing from one person (with HIV) into another person's bloodstream. It cannot get through healthy, undamaged skin. The only real risk of HIV is through anal sex without a condom – this accounts for almost all HIV transmissions between men.

Being Safe:
Even if you don't come inside someone, there is still a risk to both partners from blood (tiny cuts in the arse) and pre-come. Using strong condoms and water-based lubricant greatly reduces the risk of HIV. However, condoms can break or slip off, so:
* Make sure that condoms are stored away from hot or damp places.
* Check the expiry date – condoms have a limited life.
* Gently squeeze the air out of the tip.
* Check the condom is put on the right way up and unroll it down the erect cock.
* Use plenty of water-based lubricant (lube), up the arse and on the condom.
* While fucking, check occasionally to see the condom is still in one piece (you could also add more lube).
* When you withdraw, hold the condom tight to your cock as you pull out.

* Never re-use a condom or use the same condom with more than one person.
* If you're not used to condoms you might practise putting them on.
* Sex toys like dildos and plugs are safe. But if you're sharing them use a new condom each time or wash the toys well.

For the safest sex, make sure you use the strongest condoms, such as Durex Ultra Strong, Mates Super Strong, HT Specials and Rubberstuffers packs. Condoms are free in many STD (Sexually Transmitted Disease) clinics (sometimes called GUM clinics) and from many gay bars. It's also essential to use lots of water-based lube such as KY, Wet Stuff, Slik or Liquid Silk. Never use come as a lubricant.

Oral Sex:
Compared with fucking, sucking someone's cock is far safer. Swallowing come does not necessarily mean that HIV gets absorbed into the bloodstream. While a tiny fraction of cases of HIV infection have been linked to sucking, we know the risk is minimal. But certain factors increase the risk:
* Letting someone come in your mouth
* Throat infections such as gonorrhoea
* If you have cuts, sores or infections in your mouth and throat

So what is safe?
There are so many things you can do which are absolutely safe: wanking each other; rubbing your cocks against one another; kissing, sucking and licking all over the body; rimming – to name but a few.

If you're finding safe sex difficult, call a helpline or speak to someone you feel you can trust for support. The Terrence Higgins Trust Helpline, which is open from noon to 10pm every day, can be reached on 0171 242 1010.

Or, if you're in the United States, you can ring the Center for Disease Control toll free on 1 800 458 5231.

Rock

My arms ached. My chains were heavy and it was now six long hours since Anton, the man who had been my owner since my early teenage years, had had them fixed round my wrists and ankles. Soon, he would no longer be able to include my body as part of his property. This was to be the last time I would be whipped in this house.

I had failed to get an erection for one of Master's guests. As a result, I was to be flogged in front of the entire household. Marvin usually administered these punishments. As senior slave, he certainly could be trusted to be every bit as heavy with the lash as a freeman. Our owner only ever bothered to do the whipping personally when Marvin himself was the one tied to the post in the yard.

Marvin was some ten years older than the rest of us: in his mid-thirties I think. When both he and Master were not more than children, he'd been bought at auction by Anton's father. He must have been a bargain; the old man had always had an eye for the best boys on the market – those bargains who would grow into valuable men. Besides, the family had never been rich enough to afford the best. We had all been acquired before our prime and therefore had cost less than our present worth.

Marvin was still regarded with envy by visitors to the house. Tall and powerful with a brooding yet intelligent face, he showed few signs of his age. He had the sort of sculptured chest which, almost without thinking, people would reach out to feel – to stroke. Hair on a slave's chest was sometimes shaved off (some time ago there had been a fashion for smooth men). We who were owned by Anton had been allowed to keep ours. Marvin's caused his maleness to appear as something untamed, wild. His skin was dark, betraying his southern origin. Though he had never fought in battle, he had the air of a warrior about him. He and his father had been captured. The senior man had been sold for many times the price of his son; now the son was as valuable. Marvin had been the one who, during his puberty, Anton had experimented on – he had always been the favourite. Now, Master only wanted one man's hole to fuck, and Marvin was obedient, happy to serve and beautiful to look at.

The rest of us, in our early to mid-twenties and thus marketable commodities, were to be sold. At first we were not told of this, but we knew something was afoot. There was an atmosphere, something in the way we were treated during those last few days. We had speculated on what was going to happen to us.

Then, we were actually taken to the market. This was not unusual: slaves were sometimes valued without being put up for sale.

The market was certainly not a place for chaste thoughts. Everywhere there were young men being herded, ready to be sold. Some had been taken in war, and some had been brought by the traders who travelled to other islands, buying cheaply and making handsome profits. Others were freemen who had committed criminal acts and been sentenced to slavery as punishment.

Most of the slaves had been stripped naked, although some wore loose cloth about their waists. They were beautiful creatures; these auctions were famous for that. Sometimes ten

2

or more at once were marched through, chained one to the other by their necks and ankles. Sometimes one or two were led to the holding-pens, their hands tied in front of them, pulled along by the rope that bound them.

Whenever we were taken out in public our cocks and balls were bound tightly to give our erections more thrust, then chains would be put around our necks. These were simply to provide something to tether us with should there be need to leave us unattended. Each of us are branded with the slave's mark; even if we could have done so, it would have been foolish to try to wander. Our hands are usually tied behind our backs and our feet hobbled. There would be little chance of mistaking us for freemen.

Once we had arrived at our destination, we were taken to be examined. There was an area set aside for this: an enclosed yard where men were discussed, priced and sometimes even exchanged.

We stood obediently, the three of us in a row. Master sat on a wooden bench and waited for one of the traders to show interest.

Justin was the first to be examined. The man who approached him was half-naked. He was hairy and coarse, but obviously a wealthy freeman of some sort. He squeezed Justin's pink, round nipples slowly and thoughtfully.

Justin's nipples are very sensitive and the pressure made him squirm slightly. Like the other two of us, he had been anchored by the chained collar around his neck to a nearby post. He strained on his lead. This seemed to please the man. He patted Justin's curly, golden hair and cupped a hand under the boy's pectorals before squeezing the nipple again. He then asked our master some questions (they were muttered; we didn't hear). Master replied by making Justin bend over at the waist and inviting the man to put his finger into the waiting arsehole. Of course, we had all learnt to get well used to such invasions. Justin even tried to assist by moving his hips slowly to give the man more flesh. This too had pleased.

After making him lick the finger clean, the stranger examined Justin's mouth, his ears and his neck. He grunted in approval at the well-muscled back and the strong arms, still bound tightly behind. Then he turned his attention to Justin's cock. Justin is exceptionally well hung and gets hard at the slightest thing. The examination left him standing up like a ram-rod.

It was a proud thing on one of such low status: uncut and thick enough to choke you. His balls were tightly contracted and his golden pubes hung around them like a lion's mane. Slave that he was, he stuck his chin out in a defiant sort of way: perhaps, by this time, aware he might be taken from the other two of us, confined to a cage all night, and sold tomorrow to God knows who.

The man manipulated Justin's cock, but only a little; then he seemed to lose interest in the boy and immediately turned to Theo.

Theo is the exact opposite of Justin: short, stocky and dark. His muscles are still something to be proud of, but they are marked with dark, dark hairs all over his chest and abdomen. His cock is stubby and blunt, sticking out from a forest of black hair.

His face is still boyish and pleasant but, not unlike Marvin's, it has a wild look. Like a tamed animal: one that could still turn on you.

The man seemed very interested in Theo's arse. Theo's hairy legs are strong and his buttocks are well-formed. Many a man has wanted to be given the privilege of beating them with a strap. Theo's arse-crack is dark and mysterious. The hairs there are softer and more dense. I know that arse. I've been made to lick it often enough, and many times have had to grease it, preparing Theo to be fucked.

The man even went as far as putting some sort of implement up him. It was only a medium-sized plug, the sort which is meant to open the hole and relax it in preparation for a larger invasion. Still, it was big enough to cause Theo to go deep red. He started to breathe heavily as Master had told him to do when he found it difficult to take a guest's cock.

Then, with a nod of permission from our master, the man unbuttoned the front of his own trousers and took out his massive piece of meat. It was thick and round with a heavy, loose foreskin; pre-come was already dripping off the end. He wore a ring around the base of his balls to keep his erection as hard as possible.

He threw something on the floor in front of me and motioned for me to pick it up. It was a sheath: I knew what to do. I used my mouth to roll it over the head of his shaft. As I tasted the rubber and smelt his sweat, I began to move my lips up and down his organ. He enjoyed this, but wanted something else. He pushed me aside, making me fall to the ground. I stayed there, kneeling in the dust, thankful the chain on my collar was long enough to allow this without choking me.

Then the man stood behind Theo and, giving him a hard slap across the arse like he might a horse, he entered him. Theo almost cried out but the man clapped a hand over the boy's mouth to prevent him making too much noise. He must have been used to slaves who found it difficult to take his massive organ in one go. Despite the pain he must have felt, Theo's cock was hard. His arse, widened by the implement, seemed to accommodate every inch. Even so, the man withdrew before he came.

I was made to lick Theo's arse clean before the man turned his attention to me.

I too, have hairs on my chest, but only a few, and light brown like those on my head. There are just enough on my body to define my belly and my upper torso. My legs are sturdy, but longer than Theo's and slimmer. My cock is nothing to be ashamed of, and it was excited by the treatment the other two slaves had just received. The man stared into my face. I tried not to look directly at him nor look away: you can be whipped for either. He seemed almost tender as he traced the line of my chin.

I'm twenty-five and have always been told that I have a handsome enough face. My beard is not heavy and, in any case, my face had been shaved that morning, so my skin was as smooth as any arse cheek. My eyes are a piercing blue and this has often got me into trouble for insolence – something I never could be. I know my position and I know I am to treat any freeman, no matter how lowly, as though he owned me. It is for Master to decide who fucks me; who punishes me.

The man suddenly drew back slightly as if considering something. Then, just as I was tempted to meet his gaze, he spat in my face. The saliva dribbled down my nose and fell in drops against my chest. He spat again. This time his spit stayed in my eyebrows and almost blinded me as it made its way into my eyes. The man laughed, approving my non-reaction. He reached out and grabbed my balls which had contracted and were sensitive to his touch. He stroked them gently, just touching the hairs, stimulating my flesh and making me want to moan with pleasure.

Just as I thought he was going to be kind, he spat again and dealt me a heavy blow across the cheek. I stumbled and tried to right myself; but his hands grabbed my testicles again and pulled me back to my feet, sending a stab of pain into my stomach. The man came up close. I could feel his chest-hair against my skin. He pressed his cheek against mine and reached behind to stroke my arse and finger my hole. I wondered why he didn't make me bend over as he had Theo, but he seemed to want to test me for holding. He squeezed my body and murmured in my ear, 'Good boy! Good boy!' Then, almost fondly, he wiped some of the saliva from my face and, withdrawing, motioned for Justin to come forward and to take my cock into his mouth.

I love it when Justin is made to suck me. He's very good at it, even though I know he hates it. Justin is into girls and resents his status as a sex slave more than most. He sucks harder than Theo: he's more intense. It's as though he wants to get it over with and the best way to do this is to make you come quickly.

He set to my meat with gusto, contrasting the brutal suction with the tender use of his tongue, sending waves of desire all over my body. He licked my balls before placing his tongue gently into my piss-slit.

Then, just before I could bear it no longer, he was pulled away. The two freemen went into a discussion, which I later found out was about how much each of us would fetch when we were auctioned the following morning.

We three lads looked at each other and I couldn't help but notice Theo's worried look and Justin's slight scowl. (He knows better than to make it obvious. His back bears the marks of many correction sessions at the hands of Marvin.)

After some haggling, a price for each of us must have been decided. Of course, even if we'd known then what the purpose of all this was, we wouldn't have been told what price had been fixed upon. Slaves can get ridiculously jealous of each other if they think their neighbour is to be sold for more than they themselves are. At the time, we assumed we were merely being valued so our master would know how much we were worth.

We were finally released from the tethering-posts. Our neck-chains were linked and we were made to walk back through the market and so to home.

On the way we saw many slaves going through the same ordeal we had just undergone. Some were sulky; some clearly relished the attention being paid to their bodies. One boy was tied, spread-eagled, to a tree and was being serviced by two rough-looking lads who didn't look as though they were more than nineteen. His face was a picture of pain and lust as one and then the other abused his backside. His naked body was covered with sweat and his nipples were red and swollen.

As we passed, one of the boys yelled out to our master, 'We'll pay you for half an hour with the blond one!'

Master smiled and shook his head. 'He's already been priced. I'm selling all three of them tomorrow.'

That was the first time we actually knew. Theo looked at me and I tried to give him a sympathetic little smile. Master caught this exchange and, stopping, ran his hand over Theo's cheek. 'I'm sorry,' he said. 'I need the money.'

That afternoon, back at our master's house, I had begun to stroke my cock, finally bringing myself to an orgasm as I thought of what was in store and remembered all those other men, naked and chained. We would be auctioned alongside them the following morning. We had ceased to be men and had become 'stock'.

Master visited us later with a guest who wanted to use one of us. The man had chosen me but I was still limp – spent. It was obvious I had done the unforgivable and wanked myself. My cock is my owner's property, not mine; I knew I had no right to touch it without being told to do so. I was immediately taken to the cage.

– And there I waited to be flogged. I was told I had been awarded at least ten strokes. This might seem like a heavy punishment for what was the result of a natural impulse, but I deserved it and I knew I did. I'd only meant to feel my cock, to give myself some comfort or relief. I had tried to stop myself coming but the events of the day had been too much for me.

The metal links weighed down my arms and made it difficult for me to shift my feet. The bars of the cage were close around my naked body; I couldn't sit down. I spent the time wondering what the future had in store and who was going to buy us. I wondered whether we would be kept together or sold separately.

I remembered the young thugs I'd seen raping the slave on the tree. I wondered if they had money and were likely to end up owning my body. I almost wanted it.

I fell asleep where I stood. It seemed I was there for an eternity. Presently, a shaft of light entering the room woke me. It was Marvin and, led by a piece of rope loose around his neck, Justin. I knew what was about to happen and my cock immediately jumped. I felt a palpitation in my chest and was obscenely aware of my erection. Though I didn't look down to see it, there it was bobbing up and down. It counterweighted my balls, which contracted, making the soft, downy hairs which covered them tickle and caress the skin.

Justin was made to kneel. His hands were free and, as he had been told to, he put them obediently on his head while Marvin unlocked the door of my cage. I collapsed on the floor and kissed his feet. He used his foot to push my head away, gently but firmly.

'Stop that,' he said. 'You know what we're here for. This slave wants to piss.'

I mirrored Justin's stance, my hands on my head, kneeling. At a nod from Marvin, Justin rose to his feet, his hands still in the supplicant position. Marvin reached out and took hold of Justin's cock. It was soft but it lengthened slightly at the touch.

I did know what to do. Slaves who were being punished were often used as piss receptacles for the others. I leaned back on my thighs, opening my mouth and shutting my eyes. I didn't have to look to know Marvin was leading Justin towards me by his cock. Soon I felt the first drops of hot liquid splashing my face. We are taught how to piss, just as we're taught everything else: a spurt across the lavatory slave's face and then more on his chest. I felt the urine running down towards my navel. Justin held back and the sensation stopped for a while. Then the end of his wet penis was placed in my mouth. I closed my lips around his meat which was, by now, almost hard. I prepared myself. Justin sighed with relief and let go of the contents of his bladder.

He obviously hadn't been allowed to piss for some time; it came down my throat in a torrent, hot and salty. I gagged and tried to swallow it, but some dribbled out of the corners of my mouth. He controlled the flow and I was able to swallow what was in my mouth before he let more in. I drank and drank until his bladder emptied and his penis was withdrawn. Marvin, still holding the boy's organ, shook it and a few extra drops fell on my eyelids.

I opened my eyes, which were stinging slightly from the salt.

Justin was standing in front of me with his soft cock hanging right by my line of vision.

'Clean him,' Marvin ordered.

I leant forward and gently licked under Justin's foreskin and into his piss-slit. Before this could grow into anything too pleasurable for either of us, Marvin took hold of Justin's lead and pulled him away. Then, without another word, he motioned for me to rise. My limbs ached and I stumbled slightly as I got to my feet.

I was not to be caged again: Marvin pulled one of my wrists upwards and locked my shackles onto a ring which was secured to a beam above my head. Justin, knowing what was required of him, took my other wrist and secured it to another ring. He was then led away and I was left with his piss on my body and with thoughts of the lashing I would have to endure in a very short time.

The whipping post is in the centre of my master's yard. It is made of wood and is about six feet high. Some way before the top, chains are driven into it so the victim can be secured with his hands shackled just in front of his face.

Master sits on a chair facing the victim. He likes to watch the lash coming down on us; to see Marvin's face as he flogs us. The other slaves are made to sit behind so they can see the welts appearing and learn from the punished one's mistakes. We have to pass that post several times a day. It serves as a reminder of our position and a warning that we must always be obedient or suffer the consequences.

It was about nine o'clock by the time they were ready for me. From my prison, I could hear their voices out in the yard. This would be my last whipping in this place. From this time on, the only person who would ever be chained here would be Marvin himself, and my master would be the one holding the lash.

I was led from the house into the evening sunlight. It hurt my eyes and I squinted. Marvin fixed a heavy steel collar around my neck which forced me to keep my head up. I was taken over to Master's seat and was able to study the audience while they studied me.

Two young men, guests in our house, had been allowed to come in and watch the show. They seemed very interested in the procedure. Sitting on cushions at my master's feet, they plied him with questions.

'Is he going to be lashed now?'

'When I give the word, Marvin's ready for him. He's certainly had enough time to think about his errors.'

'Will it hurt him? Will he be marked by it?' – the older boy had a deeper voice than his brother. It made me feel strangely excited, but I also felt a tingle of fear.

'Oh, yes. A slave must be taught obedience. If you molly-coddle him, he'll not be worth selling when the time comes to do that.'

'And you're selling all three?'

'Yes, they are to be sold tomorrow.'

'Will the marks on this one's back make him cheaper to buy?' – this was the younger boy.

'No – but hush! We need to get the business over with.'

The boys were clearly impressed by my naked body. One was just below my own age, twenty-two or so, and the other some two years younger. They were alike, almost identical, but the elder one had a hard look about his face, a cruel expression. The younger seemed to pity my situation: he looked at me sadly and a little kindly.

Both of them were handsome and well-formed, their bodies tanned and muscular. They had the same jet-black hair and slightly sallow skin. Their eyes were so dark it was not possible to see if they too were black, or very dark brown. They wore loin-cloths and sandals but nothing else. They took it in turns to stroke my nakedness and examine how Marvin had tied my hands tightly in front of me. I knew Justin and Theo were standing behind me unfettered, with their hands on their heads.

The younger boy turned to Anton and asked, 'How much is he? Would we be able to afford him?'

Master laughed. 'You're not yet ready for the responsibility of a slave. Your father would not look very kindly on it if I saddled him with extra expense. A slave is like an animal. It takes feeding and housing. It's not just the cost of buying him you know.'

The young boy took hold of my genitals. 'He's so big. Will I ever be as big as that?'

'I already am,' said the other.

'No, you're not,' scoffed the first. 'I've seen your cock often enough. It's only a little bigger than mine and you're two years older than me. Mine would easily be as big as this slave's with a bit of exercise and attention.'

The elder one gave him a malevolent look: something unspoken passed between them which I didn't understand. The younger boy was cowed by whatever it was. He coloured and became very quiet. Then he stroked my cock into life and ran his other hand round the contours of my chest.

'I like hair on the body,' he mused. 'It feels so soft.'

He stroked my nipples and then pinched them. I steadied myself as he squeezed and rolled them between his fingers.

'You poor thing,' he whispered. 'You have to be whipped. I think it's going to hurt you very much.'

'What would you have me do with him?' Master asked.

The older boy replied, directing his words to me.

'I'd chain you to one of my ankles and make you crawl behind me all day. If I ever felt that you weren't keeping up, I'd use a cane on your arse. You'd suffer, but your suffering would be your humiliation. You'd have to crawl behind me everywhere – even to my college. You'd have to sit on the floor by my desk and endure the taunts of my fellow students. You'd have to follow me to the eating-house and be fed scraps from my hand. You're two years older than me at least. You'd suffer by knowing the whole town could see your master is younger than you. You, a grown man, are no more than my plaything.'

'Maybe you should own him,' Anton laughed. 'You seem to

know how to tame the beasts.' Turning to the younger one he said, 'I'll give you the honour of chaining him.'

He nodded in the direction of the post and the boy smiled. I knew he was excited – I could see his erection through his thin loin-cloth. He kissed me on the cheek very lightly and then ran a finger over my lips. His eyes met mine. I know this wasn't allowed, but he seemed to be willing me to do it.

'You poor thing,' he repeated. 'What it is to be a slave. You've been in captivity since before you were my age and you have to endure all this.' He turned to my master.

'Am I allowed to kiss him properly?' he asked.

Master seemed greatly amused by the boy's interest in me. He agreed to the request and that soft, young face met mine. He gently placed his lips against my own and opened my mouth with his tongue. His eyes, now they were close, proved to be a dark brown. His chin had not yet felt a razor. His tongue explored my mouth and I responded gratefully.

'Oh, get on with it,' his brother complained. 'I want to see how the man takes his punishment. I don't suppose . . .'

He gave a pleading look towards Anton and was rewarded with another laugh.

'You can't whip him if that's what you mean,' my master said. 'He'll hardly feel it. Look how strong Marvin is. It will take some doing to better the way he handles a lash.'

'Maybe he should have two punishments. If what I do is not enough, then give him to your slave to finish the job. I'm strong, look.'

The lad stood in front of my master and invited him to feel the biceps which were indeed remarkable. I thrilled at the conversation but, at the same time, felt utterly degraded by it. This was my position – obliged to be silent, naked and bound in front of two boys not yet out of college. They were allowed to discuss how I should be punished – how I should be tortured.

Despite these feelings I wanted Anton to say yes. I wanted this young thing to know what it was like to make me cry out in pain. I wanted him to see, one by one, the welts appearing across my back and arse. I wanted him to thrill as he drew blood from my body for the first time. I wanted to be degraded even more.

The one who had kissed me began again. This time he was more passionate and I almost tried to break the ropes which bound my hands in my desire to hold his body close to me. Eventually, I was untied by Marvin, but he held my arms pinioned behind me.

He pulled me away from my lover (for that is what I imagined him to be) and turned me around. Justin and Theo were both looking at me, Theo jealously and Justin with contempt. The display had done nothing for Justin; he was still soft. I wondered if he ever imagined women doing this to him. Theo was breathing heavily and obviously had difficulty keeping his hands where they should be. He was dripping pre-come onto the ground in front of him. It formed a spider's web between the end of his organ and the inside of his thigh. During similar sessions in the past, he had been known to come without touching himself.

Marvin, his hands now holding my upper arms close to my body, pushed me towards the whipping post and positioned me in front of it. I felt my heart leap as I saw that the boy who wanted to whip me was now holding the lash and practising swinging it through the air. His loin-cloth was full and bulging. It had slipped down his hips because of his activity. The material now cut off the thin, visible line of hair which led from his navel down his stomach to the top of his pubic area. His thighs were rippling with muscle and, for one so young, his arms were magnificent.

I felt sure Marvin was to be denied his privilege on this occasion. The young lad looked like he could easily deliver a beating which was every bit as severe as any Marvin could administer.

The younger boy was waiting to fulfill his part of the

proceedings. He was very gentle as he placed each of my wrists in the iron rings which he tightened so I could not escape.

Marvin kicked my legs apart. 'You have a choice of being gagged or not,' he said gruffly. 'If I were you I would accept. The lad looks like he knows what he is doing and you'll only get extra strokes if you plead for him to stop.'

I knew this was correct and I nodded. For some reason I was beginning to cry. It was not for fear: I had been whipped often enough before, sometimes so hard I was not able to stand at the end of it. I was full of emotion because of the boy's lips on mine and his tongue in my mouth. It had been years since I had been treated with such gentleness by a freeman. I wasn't sure what it had done to me, but I couldn't stop the tears.

Marvin glowered. 'Save them for later,' he scoffed. Then he turned to my lover. 'You can gag him too if you want, young master.'

He offered the boy a strip of rubber with a ball attached to the centre of it. The lad stood behind me and put his arms around my body. I could feel every inch of him pressing into me. His arms reached under my armpits and upwards to my face. He gently inserted a finger into my mouth to force me to open and take the rubber ball inside. Then the straps were placed around my cheeks and fastened tightly across the nape of my neck. The ball was not difficult to hold, but it was large enough to fill my mouth, making it impossible for me to move my jaw. I could bite on it. This, I knew, would help when the pain began. My lover ran his hands along the sides of my torso and gave my cock one last stroke. He put his fingers into my pubes and scratched lightly into my groin.

'I'm going to buy you,' he whispered. 'I'm going to ask my father for money and I'll buy you. I'll take care of you and my brother can have the fun of seeing you don't get above yourself. Think of that when you're enduring your punishment. It won't be the last time my brother flogs you.'

One

There was an island which had avoided the attentions of cartographers. It was not hidden, but neither was it easy to find. It was known as Illyria. Shakespeare once used its name, but this was not the place where the ship carrying Viola and Sebastian foundered, nor was it so long ago.

The island had been at peace for many years. Its armies, unpractised at the art of war, spent their days in the pursuit of pleasure, unlike their fathers and their grandfathers who had to fight to maintain the right to live as they wished.

True, not far away there were other islands and other peoples who might one day threaten the tranquillity of life here. Although these places acknowledged Illyria as being superior (certainly an unwise place to contemplate invading), there were many small realms whose sons had been taken in bondage to Illyria and were now numbered among its many slaves. Some accepted their lot. Some dreamed of a day when they would be avenged. So far no alien power had ever dared come to their aid.

There were, then, many potential threats. However, these were not omnipresent. Illyria recognised the sovereignty of some of its neighbours: some foreigners were welcome guests.

Dorian was such a person. He was twenty years old, not yet proved as a man but certainly no longer a child. His body was as developed and strong as his adoptive-brother's, despite Carlos being a full two years older.

Ignoring this development, Carlos treated Dorian as he always had done. He was embarrassed at his younger brother's presence and at their being related – even by adoption. He delighted in humiliating Dorian, punishing him for the slightest misdemeanour. Three or four years earlier, it was acceptable that Dorian should have to bend himself over Carlos's knee to be spanked. Nobody thought anything of an elder brother chastising the younger, even when a cane or a belt was used. Dorian thought this would end when he became older and stronger. He thought they would somehow become equal and Carlos would greet him as a friend. Instead, Dorian remained the smaller brother and, were it not for Carlos's increasing insistence on Dorian's being naked for his beatings, Dorian would have supposed his brother hadn't even noticed the change in his body.

The boys' adoptive father had sent them for a short visit to Illyria, where the older man had spent much of his early youth. The boys would stay with their father's old friend, Anton; it would be the end of some twelve months of travelling for them.

On the evening before they had left their father's house, he had entrusted Dorian to the 'care' of his sibling, warning Carlos he must treat the younger boy fairly.

Dorian had known their father was aware of Carlos's character. Indeed, he sometimes wondered whether the old man allowed his brother's excesses as a kind of test of endurance. He was aware their father sometimes worried his younger son might be too soft, too concerned with feelings and not enough with power.

'The best men have a balance of both,' the two had often been told.

When they eventually returned home, it would be to more

responsibility than they had had before. Despite the fact that they were not his own flesh and blood, their father would eventually hand over the running of his estates to the two of them.

No doubt he wished them to learn – he wanted each to take the best of the other and so strengthen their respective personalities.

Dorian couldn't complain. His father was a kind man and had been good to his two charges. He had taken both of them into his house when they were still children. They had been the victims of some conflict (Dorian had been too young to remember what it was). Having been born in the same area as each other and brought up in the same village, they looked very alike. They could almost have been mistaken for blood relatives. It was maybe because of this striking resemblance that they had been chosen. Dorian was thankful they were not physically related. He would not want to think he might have any of Carlos's character in his own blood.

Although they had been warned to expect a difference, the customs of Illyria had come as something of a shock to the new arrivals. They had soon realised that men here rarely, if ever, touched women in a sexual way. In fact, one barely saw a female on the streets or in the houses. (They had been told of another place not far away where all the females lived.)

'There are many places for men and women who wish to mix with each other,' their host had said. 'Of course, sexual interest here is not exclusively male to male. There are visitors, guests, traders, who prefer women and some – residents included – who like both.'

However, most of the inhabitants divided their time between sexual acts with each other and the sexual abuse of their slaves. At first this worried Dorian. He had always held an intellectual belief that a man should have the use of his own body and, no matter how or where he was born, he should have the power to decide for himself who enters him or whom he enters. This

18

was not so here. The time Dorian had spent on the island had cured him of these notions and made him see that the world was a cruel place where some must be masters and some must be slaves. Only the gods could decide which person should be which.

He was fortunate. He would be a master. Curiously, this thought did not fill him with confidence. When he closed his eyes at night, his fantasies were not of power over others, but of being subservient to bigger and stronger men. He felt ashamed of these thoughts and tried not to recall them, but when he saw a slave, naked and wretched, he ached inside, not with sympathy, but with envy.

He didn't know where these feelings sprang from. In many other ways he was proud of himself. His body was certainly nothing to be ashamed of. Twenty he might have been, but his physique would not have disgraced a man ten years his senior.

Like Carlos, Dorian had powerful arms and a broad chest. His hair was thick and curly, and one unruly black lock insisted on falling over his eyes. This gave him a sultry look which he soon found was attractive to many of the local men. His legs showed the benefits of the running he had enjoyed as a hobby since the age of ten. They were like slender tree-trunks. At their top was an arse which would not have looked out of place on a Greek statue.

Despite having good reason to be, Dorian was not conceited. He was aware of his good looks, but only so far as they were a fact he knew to be true.

Dorian and his brother were careless as to whether their beauty attracted men or women. Where they had come from, a person was happy to fuck with either sex. Here it was with men. 'So be it,' they decided.

Today they had been invited to watch the punishment of one of Anton's slaves, a magnificent specimen whose name was Rock.

Dorian wondered, as he had often done before, why the infliction of pain on another human being should be such an occasion of pleasure for the rest of them. He freely admitted to an almost obsessional interest in the ceremony. The night before he had been able to think of little else.

He had tried at first to talk about it to his brother. Dorian knew Carlos was as keen to see the thing happen as he himself was. Typically, Carlos refused to betray his feelings.

He laughed at Dorian and said, 'It's the ways of things here. If it's wrong for us to enjoy it, why do they? Even slaves that are being pissed on have erections the like of which I've never seen elsewhere. They're in their proper place all right. We might as well make the most of it while we can.' He added scornfully, 'Or does my little brother want to wipe away their tears and hold them in his arms till they feel better? They're slaves for God's sake!'

Dorian resented the tone, but he had to agree.

The time was drawing near. The slave was bound to the post and ready. He was naked, of course: slaves were seldom allowed the dignity of clothing. Dorian had secured him and this act had given him a thrill such as he had rarely experienced. There was something in Rock's acceptance of his fate, of Dorian's status over him, which gave Dorian a flickering understanding of what it was to be a master. Curiously, it also made Rock more beautiful, more manly.

His wrists were raised just above chest height. His feet were pulled apart and secured by ropes to pegs in the ground. Carlos had been given the greater privilege of carrying out the punishment. Dorian wouldn't have wanted this. He was content to watch.

Somewhere inside himself, he was aware of a secret fantasy, secret even to his own conscious, waking mind. In it, it was he who was bound to that whipping-post. It was an image which would come back to him in the days that followed.

Carlos's body was a wonderful sight. The two years he had

over Dorian had made him physically near to perfection. He was strong, muscular and arrogant.

He also enjoyed inflicting pain.

When they were younger, Carlos used to make Dorian kneel at his feet and bend his back so a lash might be used across his shoulders. When he'd done, he would make Dorian lick at his feet in order to show thanks.

Afterwards, Dorian would look at his back in a mirror and see the red stripes running across. He would keep a vivid mental picture of the beating. This picture, in some ways, was as pleasurable to him as the act itself had been. Standing in front of the mirror, he would go over every detail while he wanked himself off. Occasionally, his eyes would close as he thought of his brother: of the humiliation of being punished.

The feeling after he'd come was always one of disappointment. He wanted to hold the escalating sensation in his dick and the memory of being whipped: he wanted to keep himself in that state for ever.

Then he would feel shame. Shame at it having happened at all, but more because he felt it was wrong to relish it as he did.

Once, after such a beating, Dorian was walking down the street, his sore back covered by a loose shirt. Prior to going out, he had wanked himself off and was now adjusting to ordinary daily activities without his raging hard-on demanding attention, blocking out all other thoughts.

Across the road, where he was sitting with his friends, Carlos noticed his brother's approach. His cronies smirked when Carlos pointed and Dorian flushed bright red. It was obvious Carlos had been talking about him, about what had been done to him. Carlos's friends were all of an age, two or three years older than Dorian. They were city kids: rough, loud and aggressive. The boys' family was reasonably well off and their father would not have approved of Carlos's choice of company. Class was a great divider in those days.

What was about to happen was made worse by the fact that

a girl had also been present. Dorian didn't know why this should have added to his embarrassment, but it did. She was obviously 'with' one particular boy. He wasn't able to keep his hands off her. He constantly fondled her breasts or stuck his hand up her dress. She seemed to enjoy it. As well she might, for he was incredibly good-looking in a rough-hewn sort of way. She moaned, allowing her body to mould itself to whatever shape his hands demanded.

The other boys were more interested in Dorian. They giggled slightly, as though they were unsure of what reaction was expected of them. After all, Dorian was their superior: if not in age, at least in social rank. Carlos, as always, was determined to assert his power. He called to his brother.

'Dorian. Come here! Now!'

Dorian tried to explain he was on an errand for their father and couldn't delay. Carlos just repeated, 'Now!'

With his head down, Dorian walked slowly towards the group. Carlos made him stand before them for what seemed like an age before he spoke. He was leaning back against the body of one of the other lads, twisting some rope around his fingers. One of his legs was flat to the ground, the other slightly raised at the knee. He looked like an emperor reclining on cushions with his disreputable court around him. Dorian was his captive, miserable and ashamed, guessing at what was wanted from him.

'Tell these gentlemen what happened to you this morning, Dorian.'

Dorian could feel his cheeks burning. He hated having his face rubbed in the dirt merely for Carlos's amusement. He wanted to despise Carlos, but he couldn't. Something inside him said it was his place to be given this treatment and his brother's place to mete it out.

'You gave me a whipping,' he whispered.

'I gave you a whipping – what?' he barked.

'Sir,' Dorian replied. 'You gave me a whipping, sir.'

'Why did I do that?'

'Because you wanted to teach me manners, sir.'

What had actually happened was that Carlos had objected to Dorian's sitting in his chair in the garden. At least, he'd claimed it was his chair. It was in the best place for the sun and it was where he usually sat. On this occasion he hadn't been there and Dorian had availed himself of the prime spot. Carlos had arrived back at their villa and discovered him.

He had immediately ordered Dorian up to his room to strip and prepare himself for a whipping. Dorian had had the impression his brother wanted any excuse that day, and whatever petty infringement were discovered would have resulted in the same harsh punishment.

'Show these gentlemen the marks I've made on your body.'

Dorian really didn't want to do this, but he knew he must. Slowly, he pulled his shirt out of his breeches and eased it off his still-painful back.

The boys seemed to be interested in his chest first and foremost. One of them, a sandy-haired lad with a large mouth, pale skin and sea-green eyes, came over and ran his hand over Dorian's front. Dorian's nipples were large and dark against his skin. He felt them stir as the boy's fingers touched them. A familiar thrill spread across his chest and into his stomach. Carlos spoke sharply.

'He's not a whore, leave him. He's here to show you how I discipline my subordinates. Dorian – turn round and show your back.'

Dorian knew, of course, that his back was covered in stripes going this way and that. He had seen it in the mirror only an hour or so before. Presumably, Carlos was more careful with him than he would have been with a slave: the stripes almost never came up to flare and form welts. Unusually, this time many of them had done exactly that.

Dorian felt the boy's finger trace these marks along his shoulders and down into the small of his back. The others had gone very quiet. The girl was moaning as her lover's fingers felt inside her vagina. Dorian was utterly dejected. Even passers-by in the street, some of whom he knew, looked across. He might as well have been a slave.

Carlos came over and stood very close to him. Dorian's head was still bent but he could see his brother's chest. He did not dare look up into his face. Carlos took the younger boy's head in both hands and kissed the top of it.

'Little brother,' he said, 'you're going to be a beautiful boy for someone one day soon.'

Then he took Dorian's shirt. Dorian imagined he was about to be excused. He was. But, before he let him go, Carlos ripped the garment into four pieces. The boys laughed. Carlos let out a whoop of pleasure and fell on the ground next to one of his friends. The boy leapt on top of him and they wrestled together. Dorian watched the two for a few moments. The young muscle and smooth skin, twisting and writhing. He had been dismissed and forgotten.

He wanted to be like them: they were the very essence of masculinity. Suddenly he knew he never would be.

He knew then what he had always known secretly: that his role in life was inverted; he was a slave, forced into the life of a freeman. He wanted the whip, humiliation, chains about his feet and wrists. Fate had given him wealth and a station in life; he wanted neither. Maybe it was right that fate should also have given him Carlos as a brother.

Dorian had to return home, stripped to the waist and showing the world the marks of his degradation.

That was some time ago. He watched Carlos now, as he prepared to punish this handsome young slave. He was cracking the whip into the dust and flexing his biceps, rolling his shoulders – preparing. He was going to give the boy a lashing he wouldn't forget in a hurry.

The slave was prepared and ready. Dorian looked at the body in front of him. The buttocks were clenched in anticipation of being struck with the whip. They were hard and as firm as any Dorian had ever seen. Rock's back rippled with muscles. No doubt Anton kept his human livestock working for him. They certainly had been given no opportunity to get fat or out of condition.

The slave had short hair; he had obviously been clipped recently. It was a lightish-brown colour, which set off his deep-blue eyes. His lips were full and his mouth slightly open. He was breathing in short, panting spurts. Dorian could see his stomach rising and falling as Rock tried to control his fear. Occasionally it would tense when he held his breath; this showed off his torso to perfection – taut and sculptured. As the whip cracked unseen behind him, he let out an involuntary cry.

Dorian had a rubber gag in his hands. The slave had been given the option of having this inserted into his mouth or not. If he chose not to have it, he also undertook to take his whipping in silence. Any noises would be seen as disobedience and punished further. He had asked to be gagged.

Dorian looked around and Carlos gave him an impatient nod. Carlos was proudly displaying his chest to the obvious admiration of everyone around. He had hair in between his pecs and just underneath them: not a large amount, just enough to define the muscle. His stomach was hard and muscled. His arms, also covered in soft, dark hair, were massive.

Dorian went over to the slave and, stroking Rock's face as he did so, he inserted the gag into the captive's mouth. Rock whimpered as he did it and Dorian couldn't resist running a hand over the restrained body and down to the groin. As Dorian touched Rock's penis, the slave tried to move but the bonds wouldn't allow it.

Dorian kissed Rock's cheek and told him to take his whipping bravely. Words came out of his mouth: he didn't know where from, but in that moment he knew what he wanted out of life. It was not, as he later remembered saying at the time, to own Rock himself; it was that his brother should own the two of them together.

He retreated to the audience. Carlos took the vacant place

next to his victim. There was something beautiful in this scene. It was almost balletic. Dorian's memories of similar events were always in a sort of slow-motion. He could see every movement accentuating the very maleness of the person with the whip in his hand and also the vulnerability of the one being flogged.

This man combined his helplessness with a certain grace. In a way, the lowliness of his position and his quiet acceptance of the pain which was about to befall him made him seem stronger even than Carlos.

Carlos spared him not at all. Each lash was vicious. Sweat began to trickle down the slave's back as the stripes began to cross his arse-cheeks and his thighs.

The sound of the thin leather cracking both the air and the man's skin was enough to make Dorian wince. He had only an idea of the pain Rock must be suffering. As he knew, Carlos had always held back when punishing him. With this slave he had no need.

Carlos was sweating now; his chest was shiny with it. He wiped his eyes in between each stroke. The slave was whimpering. Strangely, to Dorian, these guttural noises sounded almost ecstatic. Even so, Rock must have been glad of the gag. Not least because it gave him something to bite upon, in order to concentrate away from the pain across his naked back.

His moans were clearly audible through the restrictive rubber. Whatever provoked them, whether it was pleasure or hurt, he would be forgiven them. Every so often, Carlos dealt him a blow which was more gentle than the rest. The slave responded to these as though they were full-powered lashes. He was slipping into that state where each crack of the whip merged into one long sensation. Soon he would be able to stand no more and his punishment would be over.

It wasn't long before the signal was given to stop the flogging. Dorian watched as the man slumped with relief, held only by the bonds round his wrists.

Carlos gave him one final swipe across the small of his back and then he stopped. Anton nodded in approval, and the boy dropped the lash and went back to his seat.

Marvin, an older slave, went over and cut the ropes which bound Rock's feet. He then released his wrists from the post and, willingly, the slave fell to the ground. Marvin knelt over the hurt body, binding the slave's hands in front of him. Then another slave was summoned: Justin, the blond, curly-haired one of the two who had been forced to watch the scene. A bucket of water was thrown over the prisoner to bring him to attention. Marvin motioned for Justin to help, and the two picked him up and dragged him away.

Rock

After being flogged, I was dragged to a cool room and left on the floor where I would be allowed to recover for the next few hours until the worst of my beating had worn off.

My lover was on my mind. When I closed my eyes, it was his face I saw in the darkness. I remembered what he'd whispered to me before the infliction of my punishment. Soon – and it was possible – soon he could well become my master. My heart beat too quickly at the very thought of it.

I had ridiculous notions of falling in love with him properly – as a freeman might love another. He would still own me, of course, but he would treat me with respect and care. I would no longer have to suffer abuse. If he were to buy me, this could be the last time I settled down for the night lying on my stomach, trying not to let the stripes across my back and my arse touch the rough ground of my cell.

Later, Theo was sent into me and he rubbed some sort of ointment over my wounds. I thought, not for the first time, how lovely he was.

There was no one about to see us. Marvin, who had brought Theo in, had tactfully retired and was waiting outside the door. He often did this, knowing full well what would happen as a result of our being alone. I think he felt sorry for us on these occasions, we victims of cruel punishments. Often a punishment meted out by Marvin himself but never easier because of that.

Theo sat upright, facing me. He leant over my shoulder to reach down my back. This meant my face was pressed into his hairy chest, just above his nipple. I licked his skin; it was salty with sweat. I noticed his cock stirring almost immediately. He left my back for a moment and leant away. I looked into his honest, boyish face, framed with soft, dark hair. I kissed his cheek. This might be the last time . . .

'Oh, God!' he exclaimed.

His cock was now rigid. He took my mouth into his, sucking my tongue deep into his throat. I returned his passion, pulling his tongue back into my mouth and creating a suction between us. I felt the back of his teeth and around his gums. He did as much for me before showering my face with kisses. Then he pushed my face away and continued his gentle attention to my back.

I locked my lips on to his nipple and sucked as a child might at his mother's breast. He ran his free hand round the top of my shoulders and then pressed my head into him. I felt secure, safe. Even the fire caused by the whip was part of this. I no longer felt I was hurting. I was truly burning: burning with sensation – on my back, in my cock, my mouth, my stomach, my heart.

Theo eased off again and, rolling on to his back, he put his legs in the air to display the soft, black hair which surrounded his arsehole. I moved towards it and began to lick in between his buttocks, finally finding his hole with my tongue. It tasted of him: musty and salty. I jabbed my tongue into it and he groaned with pleasure. I began to fuck his hole with my tongue.

'Yes,' he said hoarsely. 'Fuck me. Please, please fuck me.'

He reached over to the bag in which he'd brought the ointment. From it, he took a sheath and applied it to my cock. His touch on my organ was gentle and caressing. I could smell the rubber. I pressed myself to him and he kissed me again, this time more gently. He lay back once more and displayed his fuck-hole. I pressed my dick against it and slowly pushed. He gasped. His mouth opened and a trail of saliva began to run down his chin. I kissed it away, the movement of my body down to his face giving me the extra thrust I needed to enter him completely.

He moved with me, the two of us locked together. Theo had found his own cock. He wanked himself as he was fucked. His eyes were closed and his whole body taut with sensation. I came into him in great spurts. I came as I couldn't remember ever coming before. Was this the last time I would fill his arse? His spunk hit my chest and he let out a huge gasp.

We kissed; my cock stayed in his arse and went soft there inside him. He rubbed his come over my chest and held me tightly. The pain had passed.

Marvin was indeed making allowances, for he allowed Theo to sleep with me for an hour or so. We lay with our arms around each other and I felt the strength of his body against mine. Soon it would be evening and then night. We would be woken early the next day, ready to be taken to the market. Our fate was sealed.

'Theo!' I whispered. 'Theo, Theo, Theo.' His gentle breathing was all the reply that came back. I stroked his hair and waited.

Two

Dorian had an uneasy feeling that, despite Rock's having borne his full punishment, had he been allowed, Carlos would have dearly loved to carry on lashing his back. It was obvious how much the experience had aroused him. Carlos had stripped down to the loose cloth which they often wore round their middles as underwear. His cock was huge underneath the thin fabric, pressing against the cloth and pushing it obscenely outward.

He stood for a moment or two, panting from his exertions, sweat gleaming on his skin as his breast rose and fell. He watched as they poured water over his victim and dragged the unfortunate boy away to recover. Then, without a word, he dropped the whip, turned and ran towards the house, leaving his outer garments on the floor where he had dropped them.

Dorian picked them up and followed him. He knew Carlos had gone to his room. There he would strip naked and lie down to savour the memory of a man's back: the memory of sweat, of bondage and the whip. He would stroke himself. Slowly and softly at first, but as the scene in his mind reached its climax, so would he. Pulling on his cock with ferocious, urgent strokes, he would bring great spurts of come shooting

31

over his abdomen and chest. Then he would relax and close his eyes, allowing his dick to go soft in his hand. He would sleep for a while before cleaning his body and going to find his brother.

Dorian took the discarded clothes to his own room and waited. He lay back on his pillows and thought about what he had just seen and about Carlos wanking himself at the memory of it.

In a few moments he was asleep and dreaming. In his dream, everything was as it had been. Carlos held the whip; the other slaves knelt on the ground and Anton sat opposite. The slave, Marvin, was standing by the post waiting to tie the victim to it – but it was not the slave who was to be punished. It was Dorian himself. He felt a great sense of excitement as he stood before the assembled household, naked and aware of what was about to happen to him. His whole body shook, not out of fear but out of anticipation. He wanted it.

When he awoke, his dick was throbbing and hard. He began to wank, knowing it wouldn't take long. He was only surprised he hadn't come in his sleep.

It was not to be. He was interrupted by Carlos. In the brief pause after the knock and before Carlos entered the room, Dorian tried to cover himself. Of course, what he'd been doing was obvious. Carlos seemed to be pleased that he'd almost caught him at it.

'You enjoyed watching me teach the slave a lesson, didn't you, little brother?' he said.

'Yes,' Dorian admitted.

'He's in love with you of course. The slave, I mean. I saw the way he looked at you. I suppose that pleased you?'

His brother's tone was casual. Dorian considered for a moment before daring to voice a hope already formed in his mind. He tried to say it lightly, hoping to sound unconcerned.

'He's very pleasing to look at. I wouldn't mind owning him.'

He didn't add that he thought Rock was one of the most beautiful men he'd seen for ages: Carlos would have derided him for it. Nor did he say he was beginning to suspect his feelings for the slave went beyond a mere appreciation of his physical attributes. It was not accepted for a freeman and a slave to love one another. Even so, Dorian had always suspected such relationships were not uncommon in practice.

Even at the half-admission, his brother scoffed loudly.

'You? You couldn't own anybody. You're far too weak. You'd molly-coddle him and make him soft. He'd be worthless after a few days in your tender care.'

The word 'tender' was said with such heavy sarcasm it made Dorian angry. Still, he attempted to retain his nonchalant facade.

'I'm not like you,' he said. 'I find it difficult to be firm, but I wouldn't spoil him. You've taught me how to use discipline. I'd be careful not to allow him to take liberties. In any case . . .'

He stopped. He had been hoping Carlos would latch on to the plan which was forming in his own head. He even thought his brother would be as keen on the idea as he was himself.

'In any case – what?'

'In any case, why need I be stern with him when you are so good at – that sort of thing?'

'What sort of thing? Whipping the hide from the backs of disobedient scum?'

It took a moment or two, but suddenly Carlos's face changed as he realised what was being proposed. 'What are you saying?'

Then, even though his voice was still edged with scorn, he spoke more quietly. 'I suppose you're thinking we could own him together. You get his kisses and he gets my lash. What do I get?'

Dorian shrugged. Carlos would of course get pleasure out of meting out punishment. He couldn't deny he'd enjoyed what he'd just done to the man's body, but saying this would only anger him. He always pretended such acts were a duty, something he had to do: to Dorian; to the slave; even, on occasions, to his lower-class friends. Carlos liked to be thought of as above feelings, even feelings of lust or power.

Dorian was about to give up on his idea. Perhaps the confused emotions he felt were a result of long frustrations and not to be taken too seriously. There would be other opportunities to obtain his own man. He turned over on his bed.

Carlos stayed silent for a few moments, and then, surprisingly: 'All right,' he said.

Dorian sat bolt upright, hardly daring to believe his ears.

'You'll ask if we can bid for him?'

'I don't see why not. You're becoming a man yourself now, little brother. I can't go on chastising you for ever and I don't want to lose my touch. I need to keep up my standards of discipline so I can be fit to take charge when Father eventually leaves us.'

'We can bid for him then?'

'I'm not having you sign the papers. We'll pool the money we have but bid for him in my name only. He'll be my present to you. But . . .'

He paused, looking Dorian straight in the eye.

'But, officially, he'll belong to me. I don't want you to go weak at the knees every time he pleads with you. If you think you'll be able to treat him like sort of pet, like a lapdog, you'd better think again. He'll be ours to use. He'll have to work for his keep and he'll have to keep those muscles of his in trim. He's not going to have an easy time of it.'

Dorian nodded and swallowed hard. For some inexplicable reason, his heart was pounding. He was afraid Carlos would see his anxiety and read his thoughts.

It was true this arrangement would condemn his beautiful man to a gruelling round of punishment and hard work. Dorian had suffered under his brother's discipline himself and would hardly wish it on another, even a slave. On the other hand, it would at least give him an opportunity to keep Rock in his sights and – who could tell? – perhaps in another few years, when Carlos had tired of the novelty, he might have enough money to buy Rock and have him all to himself.

'The auction is tomorrow.' He gulped. 'Should we go and ask about it now?'

He supposed, correctly, Rock would still have to be auctioned even though the boys were such close friends of his present owner. There was, of course, no legal stipulation demanding this, but it was a tradition and they could hardly expect to get a cheap buy.

Yet this meant there was always the strong possibility of somebody else out-bidding them, even presupposing they would be given permission to bid. Dorian realised he very badly wanted to own the handsome slave. It meant something to him which he couldn't articulate or even allow to become lucid in his mind.

'Let's go,' Carlos said.

Nervously, Dorian followed him to Anton's quarters to ask permission.

Anton had finished supper. He felt ill at ease. He wasn't the type to become sentimental about his slaves. Indeed, he took the attitude that they were very much on a par with his domestic animals. He would never ill-treat them of course, but he didn't believe in becoming attached. They were his property and it was right for him to decide to sell them. Now he wasn't able to work so much he needed extra money. Some fine paintings, a few articles of furniture and three of his slaves would have to go.

Even so, he would have preferred to sell the boys privately to some friend. He would have liked to make sure they were going to a good home.

The auction was certainly the best economic proposition. His accountant had advised it and Anton didn't see why he should pay the man and then ignore the costly advice. Still, he regretted it.

Was he, he wondered, letting his feelings get the better of his common sense? After all, most men who chose to buy slaves would surely want to treat them well. Cruel handling would only reduce the value of the livestock: it wouldn't make sense.

This thought was of some reassurance, but with it came an uneasy recollection of Carlos and the delight he'd so obviously taken in lashing Rock. Anton considered punishment to be a necessary evil. He would never hold back when it was deserved, but it was not to be relished. There were many, Carlos among them, who evidently felt differently.

His troubled musings were interrupted by the arrival of his two house guests. He welcomed them readily. Both of these boys were feasts for his eyes. The evening was hot and Carlos was still stripped to his underwear as he had been earlier. The fine chest, surmounted by smooth, brown nipples, stood out proudly. His rugged legs, sturdy and covered with dark hair, stood apart. The boy exuded confidence. His brother was altogether more gentle, almost feminine. He too had a sculptured body which was temptingly evident beneath the loose, thin cloth of his tunic, but his demeanour was quieter. His jet-black hair made his face seem paler and more defined than it actually was. He kept a pace or two behind the elder boy, allowing Carlos to explain their business.

Anton wasn't surprised by their request. Indeed, this might partly be the answer to his problem. Even so, he couldn't back down on his word: the two boys would have to bid like everyone else. He told them this and, with a stern glance at Carlos, gave them a lecture on ownership and what it meant.

The boy must have known these words were meant for him in particular. He was certainly independent and confident, but he seemed almost arrogant. He didn't appear to be listening as Anton went through the list of possible problems: warning them about such things as maltreating, undernourishing or overworking the man who might soon be their new possession.

It occurred to him that Dorian seemed much more attuned to what he was saying than Carlos could ever be. Dorian's occasional, rather timid interjections made it obvious he wanted to care for the man he would own and wanted nothing more than to be a responsible new master.

Anton didn't bother to disguise what he felt. Were it not for the younger boy's presence and the assurance that the two would own Rock equally, he would have had misgivings about allowing Carlos the charge of one of his slaves.

'Punishments are a last resort,' he concluded. 'It's all very well to give slaves a light going-over to gratify your desires, but what you did today, Carlos – that should be reserved for larger misdemeanours. If you're too heavy-handed with them, it's not just cruel; it's bad management. They won't respect you and they'll become surly and unwilling.'

Carlos must have realised that his indifferent pose had been seen through. He coloured slightly but said nothing. Anton smiled at Dorian.

'I don't think I need worry as long as you have a part-share in my boy. I'm sure you might, if anything, err the other way. Just make sure this brother of yours doesn't flex those muscles of his too much, eh?'

When the boy readily agreed to this condition, Anton – although subconsciously realising Dorian had no power to have any restraining influence on Carlos – granted their request.

Anton noted the scornful look Carlos gave his younger brother and the unease crept back into his mind. He quickly dismissed the troublesome thought. Really, if he allowed such notions to cloud his business acumen, he would end up little better than a slave himself.

As soon as the boys left, Anton felt a pang of conscience. He might have just agreed to let a human being be given into the care of a powerless college boy and an evident sadist.

'No,' he told himself sternly. The auction would be the final arbiter of Rock's fate. He, Anton, wasn't to blame. It was a free country.

Still the nagging voice jabbed at his mind.

'Not for Rock,' it said.

★ ★ ★

'And how are you going to stop me using those muscles of mine too much?' said Carlos as soon as they were alone again. 'I suppose you'll complain every time you see a lash mark on his back, or a semen stain on your silken bedsheets.'

Dorian protested as convincingly as he could. 'I had to agree with Anton, didn't I? Don't worry, I won't interfere. I won't be able to – I know that.'

'Just as long as it's understood,' Carlos went on. 'Anyway, we might not get him. He might be too expensive now I've whipped his back and his arse into looking so damned inviting.'

Then, before Dorian could reply, he quickened his pace and was gone.

Throngs of people lined the streets. These were the people of Illyria: men who had built a whole culture on their love of each others' bodies. Not all of them were beautiful or young. The citizens had a place for all as long as each individual knew his place. Every six months or so, a new ship would pull into the small bay with new arrivals of freemen.

These, mostly boys and young adults, would be schooled in the way of their predecessors. They would mostly have come from nearby friendly islands, but some were from the mainland which, like an indulgent father with his child, tolerated and indulged the Illyrian way of life. The mainlanders would allow any man or boy who wanted to live on the island to do so and yet remain under their protecting laws. Like the Illyrians, they too were a conquering race and their enemies would also be sent here: in chains, across to the bay where they would presently begin their lives of slavery.

Market days were a favourite monthly event, and this was to be a special one. Today, the annual auction would take place. Instead of private deals, usually agreed between one owner and another in the market taverns or in the surrounding streets, a podium had been erected in the centre of the main square, ready for the mass selling of captive males.

Some way away, these unfortunate men awaited their fate.

They were kept in another, smaller square. The ground was studded with small tethering-posts in front of which were smooth wooden phalluses, each about the size of a large cock. A slave would be made to kneel back on his heels in front of one of these. His arse would then be impaled. This done, he would be chained to the post by a loose metal collar round his neck. His hands would be secured behind him. Lastly, his cock would be bound tightly with twine. He would not be allowed to relax this position until he was given permission, and such permission would only be granted when a potential buyer decided to take a closer look at his body.

This square was beginning to fill with livestock. Each man to be sold had been given a reserve price and this was written on the back of his shoulder blade so he couldn't see it.

They were well spaced in the square: a good four feet surrounded each one. This allowed the purchasers to walk around them and examine any part of a slave which might be of interest. Should a buyer wish to test further – with a fucking or a whipping, for example – a small fee was payable to the market's landlord. Many who had no intention of buying would avail themselves of this privilege. Thus, the slaves were used as cheap whores. It was the way of things.

Dorian and Carlos approached. They had with them a small pouch containing what they hoped would be enough money to buy the slave they wanted.

Market day was just beginning.

Rock

The thing filling my arse had ceased to hurt me. Sometimes I forgot it was in me and reminded myself by moving slowly up and down on it. The sensation was pleasant now, but it hadn't been at first. The market workers don't allow us to adjust to such things slowly. I had been impaled on the over-large wooden dick in a matter of seconds. Before I had time to recover from the shock, I had been manacled and my slave-collar had been chained to a post. Theo was a little way away from me, and Justin had been placed further to my right. I could tell Theo was accepting the situation as I was myself. He had received quite a lot of attention from various men and had been made to suck one or two off. Neither of us had been taken away from the square.

Justin had been taken to be used. He'd been away for about two hours. The man who had taken him had made no secret of the fact that he didn't want to buy him, merely to fuck him and, perhaps, to see how he reacted to various forms of mild torture.

He was an older man, in his thirties. He had paid particular attention to Justin's blond pubic hair and also to his nipples. He had seemed pleased when he discovered how sensitive these were. The requisite fee had been paid and Justin had been led off. As he walked past me, he gave me a glance which told me exactly what he was feeling. I often wondered if he might cope better were he to be sold as a slave to a female. Was it the slavery he hated or other men using his body?

He was eventually dragged back, supported by two market workers. He had been beaten, and his arse glowed bright red. I supposed he had been fucked as well. He was placed back on the phallus, but this time he didn't wince as it went into him. Evidently, his hole had been stretched by the man's cock. He hung his head, his golden hair hiding his flushed face. He was shamed; he didn't want to meet my eye. I felt sorry for him and turned the other way to give him some respect.

He wasn't left in peace for long. A boy of maybe twenty, rich, tall and, although not conventionally attractive, pleasant looking, stopped by him. He knelt down, putting his hand under Justin's chin. He raised my friend's head so their eyes met.

'Nice!' he muttered.

He reached down and took Justin's cock between his fingers. Despite his leanings, the feel of anybody's touch on his penis would make Justin hard almost at once. He wouldn't have been allowed to come during his earlier ordeal: it was not considered good form to give the slaves release. It might cause them to be soft when they came up for auction.

The boy massaged Justin's cock until it stood out at its full length. He leant into Justin's face and kissed him for a long, lingering, thirty seconds. Justin didn't like being kissed, but of course he had no option but to respond. The market workers patrol around and, if they see a slave not doing his best for a potential customer, that slave will be punished extremely severely. At last the boy withdrew. He walked around Justin, paying a lot of attention to his arse. He even made Justin fuck himself on the dildo, commanding him to move up and down it slowly while he watched the hard wood pushing into the already sore hole.

Then he smiled in an approving manner. I thought he was going to pay to use Justin for an hour or so, and I hoped he would be gentle with him.

Instead the boy had a word with one of the market workers. He made a note on a piece of paper and walked away. If this man was going to be Justin's new owner I hoped he would be a kind one.

Three

The market was a truly incredible place. Dorian had never seen so many townspeople in such a state of anticipation. Unusually, there were more than a few women dotted about in the crowds. He didn't know whether, like himself, they were there to bid or whether they had come over as spectators. The men grouped together. Some boasted of their wealth and said confidently which purchases they were about to make. Others, presumably with less money, made discreet enquiries, hoping the man of their choice would not be in somebody else's sights.

Slave auctions were not frequent events. Dorian seemed to remember hearing they were held every twelve months or so. Not every household goes to buy or sell. Many are there simply to enjoy a day out. There was certainly something of a fairground atmosphere about the square. Traders mingled with the crowd, selling leashes, whips and flesh-clamps. Others sold food and drink.

The two brothers walked around the place where the slaves were kept prior to the auction. By the time they arrived, Rock had already been removed. This meant he would be sold early in the proceedings.

Even with the first batch gone, there seemed to be an awful lot of human flesh to be had and most of the reserve prices were surprisingly low.

The brothers took some time to meander around the stock. Dorian feared Carlos might change his mind and suggest they buy somebody else.

He seemed particularly interested in a rough-looking boy of about seventeen who looked like a farm labourer. He had sandy hair which was cut short and large, brown eyes like those of a young colt. The lad's skin was tanned by the sun and his square jaw and broad shoulders told of hard physical work. He had strong, thick legs with muscled thighs leading to small but wonderfully formed buttocks. His wrists and forearms were developed beyond his years and his upper chest filled out handsomely as he breathed in.

Attractive, yes. But not to be compared with the one Dorian was already thinking of as his own.

Carlos took the boy's penis in his hand and rubbed the tender head, pulling back his foreskin in order to do so. The boy drew in his breath and remembered, just in time, to look downwards.

'He's better value,' Carlos commented. 'But I suppose you're still stuck on your first choice.' He didn't wait for Dorian to answer. 'Stand up,' he ordered the lad.

With some difficulty, the boy stood. To his evident relief, his arse slowly expelled the wooden thing on which he'd been impaled.

Yes, his body was magnificent, but practically all the livestock were like that. True, there were 'bargains' some way off, but not many people seemed interested in them. They were the ones who were out of condition or not physically beautiful. They would be snapped up as household servants and would possibly have a better time of it than those whose best selling-points were their bodies.

Carlos took off his belt and struck the boy across the backside. The slave didn't flinch. Carlos repeated the action. Dorian noticed the boy bite his lip slightly. He worried, not for the first time, about his brother's sadistic streak.

'Come on,' Carlos said to him. 'I'm teasing you. I don't want him, he's too strong-willed. He'd be trouble.'

Dorian thought they were about to move on but, before they did, Carlos reached behind the boy and inserted a finger into his arse.

'Nice though,' he commented. 'How old are you?' he asked the slave.

The boy looked slightly panic-stricken. He looked firmly at the ground in front of him. Carlos lifted the strong chin so the boy's eyes met his own. Then he struck him across the face causing the cheek to flush red. The boy's eyes filled with tears and he tried to turn away. Carlos wouldn't allow this. He pulled the boy's face round again.

'I asked you a question,' Carlos said quietly. 'How old are you?'

'Perhaps he doesn't know,' Dorian ventured.

'Stop interfering,' Carlos snapped. 'I won't take insolence from a teenager who's about to be sold on the open market.' He struck the boy again, this time across the other cheek. The blow brought corresponding colour to the other side of the slave's face. He gasped, but did not speak. He steadied himself and lowered his head as if this might prevent his being struck again. Then he muttered something without opening his mouth properly. Carlos appeared to be enraged by this apparent insubordination. Just in time, the man in charge of the stock drew close to them.

'Having trouble, gentlemen?' he asked.

'Nothing I can't handle,' Carlos replied. 'I merely wanted to know the age of this piece of filth, but he seems reluctant to talk.'

There was an awkward pause. The man in charge took Carlos by the arm and led him a few paces away from the terrified-looking boy.

'He can't talk,' the man said. 'He's not allowed to show

customers in case it affects the price we get for him, but I'll tell you myself – he can't talk.'

'What? He's dumb?' Carlos said.

Dorian could almost hear him add, 'Why didn't he say so?' but Carlos stopped himself just in time. The information sank in. Hiding his feeling of foolishness, he recovered his usual scornful demeanour.

'What use is a slave without a tongue?' he joked. 'Do you expect me to use my brother's mouth to clean my backside?'

'He has a tongue, but he can't talk,' the man explained patiently. Carlos ignored him.

'Come along, Dorian. We'd better find your favourite piece of meat.'

Dorian looked back at the young lad, standing there, head bowed, legs apart – beauty in chains. Tears were falling on the ground before him. Not for the first time, Dorian realised how much freemen were responsible for those whom they owned. He wanted to apologise to the boy, but he knew this would be seen by one and all as a ludicrous thing to do.

Carlos followed his brother's gaze. A cruel smile hovered over his lips.

'He might not be able to form words,' he sneered, 'but I'd get some sound out of the bastard.'

In the centre of the market was a podium where, in turn, each of the men and boys who were about to be sold would be paraded in front of the eager crowd. The customers who were now thronging into the place ranged across the social scale. At one end of the class divide there were the older, calmer owners: those who appreciated the beauty of a human body as they might a good wine. Often these people arrived in pairs: lovers, or just friends who liked to discuss the merits of this torso against that pair of legs. These people usually had more money to spend than their younger counterparts and would, no doubt, be the toughest bidders. They kept their stables of slaves – thoroughbreds to a man – as signs of their standing in society.

Most were dressed in fine linens and silks. The weather was hot and occasionally a scent of perfume would drift into the air as a couple of them swept past.

At the other end of the scale were the village lads with just a few discs to spend. They would be interested in the thorough-breds too, of course, but most of those specimens would be out of their price range.

These boys wore tunics, or were bare-chested. Those slaves whose sexual inclinations went towards young men would hope to be bought by such as these and, if they were, would regret it later. Although the richer and older men were not so attractive, their demands tended to be less arduous and they would normally treat their property much more respectfully than the younger, poorer citizens.

Although of a higher class, Carlos might have fitted into the lower group: a young and good-looking master who wanted a body to fuck, to whip, and to abuse. He, like a good many others, cared little for the feelings of the man he was to buy and would think nothing of it if his investment was worn out in just a few years' time. On the other hand, a slave who was sold to a high-class stable would be fed well, cared for, and be made to fuck with other slaves who were as attractive as himself. Most of the older owners were voyeurs and needed only a few minutes' attention to gratify their physical needs.

There were, inevitably, exceptions to both these types. Dorian looked at a rich, older man standing near him who was talking in a loud voice about the gruelling punishments he gave his boys: 'I had him hanging by his wrists. It's amazing to see the look on a youth's face when you approach his arse with a cock the size of mine. He tried to wriggle away but, of course, he could do very little. I applied myself to his arse and that tight hole is something I'll remember for some time. I let him think it was over before I fucked him again. Sometimes I get these moments of pity, but not often. I've left him spread-eagled in the courtyard with a truncheon inside him. If his body ejects it before I return, he'll spend the next few hours contemplating having my dick up him for most of the night. He knows who his master is all right.'

Dorian shuddered at the man's vulgarity. Maybe he himself was an exception to type.

From his place at the front of the stage, the chief auctioneer would keep his eye on the prospective owners and decide when the bidding was over. By now, the first of the livestock to be sold would be ready.

Dorian could only imagine the atmosphere in the cell beneath the square where the slaves awaited their turn to be presented for sale. Something like two hundred men, all of them nervous, would be crowded together in a space about thirty foot square. Most of them would be aching to relieve their hard cocks. They had had the best part of a day being examined, rubbed, some of them fucked. None had been allowed to come. Some may have ejaculated accidentally and would, no doubt, be punished for having done so. A soft cock reduces the price of a slave by huge amounts and is never tolerated, even when caused by nervousness.

Dorian thought about Rock, there in the midst of them, not knowing who his new master was going to be. Carlos reminded his brother several times that their money was limited. If the bidding went higher than two hundred (not an enormous sum), then they would have to bow out. If that proved to be the case, he had suggested they might consider buying somebody else, but Dorian wasn't interested. Carlos only wanted a piece of meat, something to hurt. Dorian wanted the look he had seen in his man's eyes. He felt the warm glow spread through the pit of his stomach again. Though the realisation was tinged with a certain shame, he felt the pleasure of being in love.

The chattering and general movement in the square was at its height. The auctioneer had already mounted the stage and was going through his papers. He was a slim man in his mid-thirties. He wore a loose gown under which a lithe, toned body could easily be imagined. He had a kindly face; Dorian was glad of that for the slaves' sake.

He wondered if this man ever exercised discretion, perhaps turning a blind eye to the higher bidding of a customer who looked cruel or loutish. Dorian decided he might well be the sort to do just that.

He had positioned himself at the front in a place where he could see Carlos, who was standing some rows back. They had decided to bid separately so as not to let their interest in Rock be known. Such keenness usually betrayed a prior knowledge of something special about the lot. It encouraged other bids and resulted in higher prices.

Presently, a bell was rung and the buzz of conversation dropped to whispers. Then there was silence. The auctioneer banged his gavel on the table in front of him and welcomed the citizens of Illyria to the twenty-first auction of slaves to be held since their founder had hit on the idea in the early years of the colony.

The first to be sold off were those who would most likely go into domestic service. Most were not going to be of much use in a bedroom, either because of their looks or because of their age. Having said that, some people preferred their men to have a bit of bulk about them, or got their kicks out of fucking older, less classically beautiful men.

One such slave, who was overweight but not unattractive because of it, did go for a remarkably high price. He was perhaps in his late twenties and had probably come from an indulgent owner who had allowed him to eat too well. His eyes were a cool green and his body was sturdy, showing that a little work might turn his girth into muscle. His chest was covered in light-brown hair and his cock was enormous. During the bidding for him, the auctioneer made him bend over and display the hole in his arse. (The men on the stage were chained loosely from wrist to wrist and by their ankles. This allowed them enough movement to display their bodies as required.)

A youngish, red-headed buyer, who seemed nervous, was

very keen to get him. The price rose as several others in the crowd realised the potential of the body on display. When the hammer came down, a cheer came from the group who surrounded the redhead. It was clear the man's new master was going to make sure his money was not wasted.

There was a short break after the stock of 'servants' had been exhausted. Most of the remaining buyers had already earmarked the goods they were interested in and were now preparing to do business with others who wanted the same as they.

Dorian mused on how many people had tested Rock and how many were as determined to buy him as he was himself. Rock had already been taken to the cell under the podium and was therefore going to be sold early in the day.

To give him his due, Carlos was being helpful in this matter. Dorian realised his brother cared little which man they eventually came home with but knew Dorian did. He'd taken care to give them a good chance of obtaining their prize. To this end, he had advised Dorian to put a few 'hopeless' bids in for the preceeding sales. This, again, was to put others off the scent.

The auction proper began with a very popular lot. He was about eighteen and looked proud and stubborn. This can be a bad trait, but some buyers would seek it and even pay over the odds for it. It was generally supposed the slave had only recently begun his life of servitude. He needed sharp and sometimes painful slaps across his face and arse before he would move into the required positions to show off his young body. A group in the crowd offered loud comments. They presumed he was a recently taken captive and still thought of himself as a freeman with rights. This apparent conceit was treated with much derisive laughter.

His torso was almost hairless. It was possible he had been shaved, for his legs were covered in a thick, downy hair. His forearms, too, were hairy, leading to large biceps and rippling shoulder muscles. A lot of the slaves had had their hair cropped closely, but this one had been allowed to keep his long, brown locks. They framed his face, giving it a gentle appearance, despite the glint of revolt in his piercing eyes.

When he turned for the first time, an appreciative cheer went up from the crowd. His back was a mass of recent whip strokes, showing his lessons in subservience had already begun. As Dorian had feared, this increased the bidding sharply. The boy's back reminded him of Rock's. Although neither of these slaves was scarred, the remnants of Rock's punishment might well still be evident.

The boy was bought by one of the connoisseurs and Dorian was glad for him. His transition from prisoner to slave would be easier in such a household.

Two or three others followed; each had a body to be proud of and each was enthusiastically received. Dorian felt compassion for the frightened ones. They tried to be obedient, tried to do what they must, but they were terrified. He hoped they would go to kind masters.

After a while he recognised one of Anton's boys – the dark, hairy one. He was also popular with the crowd. Before the bidding began he was made to stroke his own penis until he almost came. As the slave's breathing became heavy and his body tensed, the autioneer pulled the hand away and used a belt across the lad's arse-cheeks to bring his attention back.

Theo, for that was his name, stood obediently, his hands, linked by chains, at his sides. He tried not to look at the faces of the men who clamoured to buy him.

The winner was another of the thoroughbred owners. He was a cheerful-looking man who was leading another slave by a leash. He treated this boy as a sort of pet, stroking and patting him every so often.

Theo had gone for an astounding eight hundred discs. Dorian had been foolish to think their savings would be enough. Rock was easily as valuable as this one and they hadn't had nearly enough money to make a realistic bid for him. Previously Dorian had hoped, expected, the prices would hover around the reserve amounts. Clearly, this wasn't going to happen.

He looked across at Carlos, who wasn't looking back: he was playing with his cock under his tunic. He might well have already given up on the idea of owning an expensive boy. Once Rock had been sold to somebody else, Carlos would be content to spend their money. Perhaps he would want to buy a younger man: one who would not fetch such a high price because of the time and effort it would take to bring him to full potential.

Dorian couldn't concentrate on the next two lots. They were both very pleasing to the eye and both very popular with the crowd. The only thing Dorian was interested in was the price they went for. In each case his heart sank. One went for seven hundred, the other for seven hundred and fifty.

It was time. The previous sale was completed and the naked boy was led into the hands of his eager new master. The auctioneer silenced the hubbub.

'Now for lot number five. He is twenty-five years old and his name is Rock. His last owner has three of his boys up for sale today and, as I said when his last offer was put before you, all three are exquisite. This one, I'm told, is obedient and has an even temper. He will delight the most demanding of men in every way and has been trained to the high standard we would expect from such a distinguished citizen as his present owner, Anton. If any of you wishes any part of his body to be presented in a special way, you have the usual three minutes to make your wishes known.'

He was led on to the stage. His body had been oiled, or maybe he was sweating. In any case, his skin gleamed in the sunlight. His light-brown hair was clean and shining; his sharp, blue eyes looked calmly ahead; his wonderful chest thrust out in a proud manner. He was taking care to keep his stomach taut in order to accentuate the shape of his body. His cock was almost hard; his hands, chained as they were, rested by the upper part of his thighs. He was having to make some effort not to touch his dick. His back still bore the fading marks of his punishment at Carlos's hands. Several people in the crowd pushed forward. Dorian looked towards Carlos, who nodded as if to say, 'Here we go.'

Before the bidding, several requests were shouted out. Nobody could seriously believe these had anything to do with the business of selling him.

'Make him bend over. I need to see his arse.'

'Tell him to pull his foreskin back.'

'What does he look like when he kneels with his head bowed?'

'Pull on his nipples. Let's see how sensitive they are.'

Rock obeyed each command. When his nipples were given a savage tweak he opened his mouth very slightly and drew in air sharply. His cock lengthened immediately. This provoked a cheer from several parts of the audience.

The bidding started at eighty, but quickly rose into the hundreds. Carlos put in two offers, while Dorian stayed quiet. Waiting for the time when he would have to bid what they could afford. Truth to tell, he had already given up. It was obvious that Rock would be sold for as much, if not more, than the others who had gone before him.

Rock

We were like so many frightened cattle. The cell we were in was hardly big enough for half our number. There was no room to sit down or even to squat.

We'd been forced into the room in some sort of order. Those who were to be auctioned first had to wait to go in so as to be near at hand when their turn came to be sold.

We were the second group of the day. Others still waited in the yard outside. More still were yet to be brought to market. I couldn't help wondering what it would be like at the end of the day, when the very last man would be waiting all alone for his turn.

As we were hustled towards the cell, I was relieved to be held back until quite near the end. This at least meant I wouldn't have long to wait before I would know what my fate was going to be. It also meant I was near the door and at least had a breath of air: there was a small opening, high in the wall above the entrance to the cell.

After so long having our bodies examined, caressed and abused, most of us were desperate for sexual release. Even the straight ones, Justin included, sported full erections. Justin had glanced at me as he was pushed past and into the cell. It was a look I knew well. It meant that showing his hard-on was not something he took pleasure in. He would rather his scowl was taken as the measure of his feelings, of his contempt, for all around him, including his fellow slaves. Unfortunately for him, this very attitude was highly prized. Some freeman was going to revel in taming him, as he might with a stubborn but beautiful horse. He was one of the few blonds amongst us whose skin was not pale, but golden brown. He would surely be snapped up in minutes.

Justin had never appreciated how well off he had been with our master. Although he had been made to have sex with other men and this was against his nature, he had not been used half as much as we others whose inclinations were different and were more likely to take pleasure in what we were made to do.

Theo stood quietly, his body hair capturing beads of sweat on his chest. He looked towards the ground, apparently lost in his own thoughts. He appeared calm and resigned. Theo – who never complained, who never asked for more than he was allotted and who took every trial in life as willingly as though it were merely a change in the weather. His Italianate looks were also going to be highly marketable.

The close proximity of so many other naked men did nothing to calm our ardour. Of course, none of us dared touch ourselves. We even tried to avoid brushing up against the other slaves for fear of an involuntary ejaculation. Needless to say, avoiding such contact was impossible.

I tried hard to think of other things, but at the same time was careful not to lose my hard-on completely in case I would be punished for having a soft dick. Justin was somewhere near the middle of the room. Theo, on the other hand, was now standing reasonably near to me, closer to the door than I was.

I regarded my old friend, taking in his handsome face and muscular, hirsute frame for what might be the last time. Still he looked at the ground, although I was able to detect he was getting nervous.

Although our fetters were long enough to allow us to move,

the space around us was not so accommodating. Theo was next to a dark-skinned youth – possibly from the East. This boy had a face which seemed older than the rest of his slim body. It was handsome, but looked incredibly serious. His jet-black hair was slightly greasy and fell straight across his forehead. His nose was slightly too large, giving his face a fetching, lopsided appearance. I could see from his intense concentration and from his body movements that he was rubbing his dick against Theo's thigh. Either he didn't know what was expected of him or he didn't care. His black eyes were fixed on Theo's face. Theo looked determinedly downward and away from him. The youth was pressing more and more urgently; his breathing was heavy. It would not be long before he came. I wondered how long it would take him to get hard again. It was possible he could do so without much difficulty and so could afford this indulgence.

He wasn't the only slave taking advantage of his neighbour's body. I could feel the hot, sweat-dampened spot where the man behind me was pushing himself into the crack between the cheeks of my arse. I let him go thus far but was ready to pull away at the least attempt to enter my hole. His dick felt good against my backside and I was tightening my buttocks, gripping it, holding it there. The man pressed against me, all hot breath and passion. He kissed my shoulder and nuzzled into my neck.

'Take care,' I whispered. 'Our bodies do not belong to us.'

Occasionally there was a gasp as somebody or other orgasmed. Other than that, but for the clank of our chains and the sound of our breath, there was an eerie silence.

After what seemed like an age, the first of our number was pulled out of the room and marched away. The atmosphere changed. Maybe it became more intense. It wasn't anything that was discernible, but the change was there all the same. Almost as soon as this had happened, an official entered the cell and sorted two or three from the group nearest the door.

'As soon as that one is sold, you are next,' he said curtly. 'Come with me. I'll put you in order of sale outside.'

He led them out of the room. This meant those of us near the door could move into the space they had vacated. In some ways this was good. We had more room, but it also, presumably, meant that we would be next up. I was glad to see Theo was still close to me. There was a hope, a fleeting chance, we might be sold to the same bidder. He looked at me and gave a half-smile. I noticed the come from the Indian drying on his upper thigh.

I could also see that the Indian, who was still with us, was already getting hard again. He was now looking towards the boy on his other side, about to rub himself off again. His intended target gave him a fierce look and edged away slightly.

The dark-skinned youth gave up on the idea and stood with his head bowed. His now fully hard dick was standing proud. His fingers moved towards his pubic hair. He began to stroke it, sometimes cupping his hand under his balls. I noticed he avoided his cock: he knew how far he could go. He saw me watching him and gave me a dazzling smile. He really was good-looking and seemed to be quite at home with his situation. I sent up a mental prayer that he would find a good home.

It was some time before the keeper appeared again. As expected, he selected myself, Theo, the Indian, and a couple of others to be taken next.

We were led into a long corridor from where we could hear the sounds of the auction going on above us. Though they seemed some way away, and we couldn't hear the actual words which were being spoken, we got the sense of excitement and could make out the cheers as the hammer went down after a sale.

At the end of the corridor was a barred gate leading to stairs. It was through this that we would be taken, up the stairs to a small room where we would await our turn on the platform. I could make out the feet of the men in the previous group. Every so often, the keeper's sandals would appear as he selected the next to go.

Theo had managed to place himself next to me.

'I'll miss you,' he said.

'And I you,' I replied.

He looked around to make sure none of the masters could see. We slaves were alone in the corridor. He pressed his mouth against mine and, for what was going to be the last time, I allowed his tongue to enter between my lips. His hands came up to the sides of my face and I felt the cold metal of his chains against my chest. I placed my arms around his body; I was almost able to hold him, but my fetters stopped me just short of the centre of his back. Our groins met and I felt the burning of his genitals against my own. We kissed for a long time, our tongues running around each other's mouths. Theo had his eyes closed. I kissed his eyelids and his nose. He pressed his cheek against mine. I realised how close we had become.

The Indian boy looked at us hungrily as we kissed. He edged towards us and stood inches away, watching intently. Very slowly, he came closer. We were aware of him, but ignored his presence. It wasn't long before I felt a hand brush against my cock. I moved slightly out of reach but he came even closer. He had Theo's cock in his other hand now. I watched for Theo's reaction: he was oblivious, more interested in our own lovemaking. The Indian was standing between us, his dick pressed together with ours. His lips met our lips. We kissed three ways, exchanging our hungry mouths one for another. The Indian felt towards my nipples. His fingers squeezed the tender flesh – he was doing as much for Theo at the same time. Theo's chains had warmed against the heat of my body; the Indian's were cold. I reached across and felt between the boy's legs. His penis was wet at the end. I stroked it downward towards his pubes. He groaned slightly. Theo moved his own cock into my other hand and I brought the two of them together, using my hand to massage them against each other. The Indian was feeling inside Theo's arse. Theo was moving slowly up and down, letting himself be fucked by the boy's fingers. We were being reckless, but the sensation was too much for us and we had to continue.

The others were looking on, fearful but aroused. Several of them had their eyes towards the barred gate, looking for the approach of our keeper. One was brave enough to come close to us and tentatively feel across the cheek of my arse with his hand. I responded by pushing my backside towards him. He retreated and stood a few paces away, watching.

By now, the Indian was wanking himself. His strokes became more and more urgent and his stomach tensed as his orgasm approached. Theo, who had taken care to keep his own hands off the Indian's cock as soon as he knew there was a danger of his coming, gently tried to stop the boy before it was too late. He pulled the lad's hand away, but the other shook his head briefly and immediately went back to his cock.

When he came, I marvelled at how much spunk he could produce considering he had come only a few minutes ago in the holding cell. Great spurts of white come spattered both our naked bodies. The Indian gasped as if he hadn't had relief for years. He grabbed us in turn by the back of the neck and took one last hungry kiss; sucking hard into the insides of our mouths. Then he pulled away and stood by the wall. He used his own spit on his hand to clean his dripping cock. We scraped the come off our bellies. There was silence all about us.

Theo was taken before me. The keeper came for him, yanking his arm and pulling him up the steps. He was rough and Theo almost lost his footing. He looked back at me, a desperate expression on his face.

I tried to smile but felt too sad. I was angry at the keeper's brutal treatment of my friend. I seldom felt that way for myself, but I couldn't bear to see Theo being pulled out of my life as though he were a piece of meat. I suddenly felt very protective towards him. I wanted to put my arms around him again and make everything all right. The most I could do was hope he would be sold to a master who would look after him and not treat him badly.

Life seemed very harsh at that moment. I had, long ago, accepted my status as a slave. It was only occasionally, when somebody kind and gentle like Theo was in danger, that I resented our lot.

I thought, too, of Justin, who was still waiting below in the middle of the crowd in the holding cell. I knew he could look after himself. In any case, we had never been very close. Naturally I hoped for the best for him, but it was Theo I ached for just then: he suddenly seemed very vulnerable. I felt tears on my face. I was crying.

The Indian came over and laid a hand on my shoulder. I looked at him and smiled weakly.

'He was your lover? Yes?' asked the boy.

I shook my head. 'A friend. A very lovely man.'

'It is possible you will both be sold to the same man. It sometimes happens. If not, fate will see to it that you are together again one day.'

He patted my shoulder and I nodded and smiled again. He retreated and stood by the wall again. Incredibly, his cock was already beginning to lengthen yet again. Was the situation we were in arousing him? Or was it just that he had an insatiable appetite? Whatever the case, he was fortunate to be able to get an erection so easily: I was relieved for him that he would not be punished for wanking himself off.

A cheer could be heard from up above us. Theo had been sold.

My turn came at last. I was manhandled up the stairs. The keeper opened the gate with his great bunch of keys and I was suddenly blinded by the brilliant sunshine. I was positioned on the centre of a kind of rostrum. The keeper kicked my legs apart and roughly slapped my face into a position where the buyers could see my features.

My heart leapt. There, near the front, was the boy whom I called my lover. His dark eyes, one partly covered by a lock of coal-black hair, were fixed intently upon me. For a moment I hoped he was there to make a bid for me, but that was impossible. Still, I remembered his words whispered in my ear before his brother whipped me.

'I'm going to buy you. Think of that when you're enduring your punishment. It won't be the last time my brother flogs you.'

It was too much to hope for.

The auctioneer invited the audience to position me as they wanted. I was made to do this and that: bend over, stroke my cock, pull my arse-cheeks apart to display my hole. The auctioneer put his fingers into my arse; he squeezed my nipples hard. The crowd seemed pleased with what they saw. I tried to make my mind a blank. Humiliation of this kind had been with me since I was in my late teens. My body belonged to whoever owned me. I had no right to any dignity I might secretly crave.

The bidding eventually began. I couldn't help but look towards my lover. He did make a bid, but it was way down at the start and he quickly seemed to give up. Soon the price for me had risen into the six hundreds, the seven hundreds, eight, nine . . .

Suddenly I resented all this. What right had they to sell another human like an animal? Why had fate given them the licence to humiliate me? For centuries, men had covered their bodies with clothes. Why was I denied this? What had I done to the gods that they should decide I spend my life in chains and naked?

I was eventually sold for nine hundred and fifty discs. My old master would be pleased.

I couldn't see who it was that had bought me. It was somebody at the far end of the crowd. I was pushed off the stage and made to crawl on my hands and knees behind an assistant who would lead me to my new owner.

Four

'What do you want to do?' Carlos asked. 'It's partly your money, so I suppose you have a voice in what it's to be spent on.'

'I don't know,' Dorian replied.

Rock had been sold for much more than they could afford and Dorian suspected any remaining men who were halfway decent would attract similar prices. Had it not been for his feelings towards Rock, he wouldn't have dreamt of spending money on a slave just yet. He could get whatever sex he wanted easily enough and he hadn't Carlos's predeliction for hurting and humiliating others.

The cheaper lots had long gone, sold off at the beginning of the auction, and, even if they hadn't, none had interested Dorian in the slightest. Their only chance of buying anything now was to wait until the very end of the day when most of the people in the crowd had bought what they wanted and the competition would not be as fierce. There might be the odd bargain to be had.

Dorian's feelings for Rock were such that it seemed to him like a kind of disloyalty to bid for somebody else. He knew this was a ridiculous emotion. There was nothing he could do to win his prize. The man he had set his heart upon had been sold and was probably, even now, being instructed in his new life.

'You're pathetic,' Carlos said. 'He was only a slave for God's sake. There are enough others who would suit us just as well.'

'Suit you, you mean,' Dorian replied.

'If I have to go home empty-handed, it will be you who'll suffer for it. If there's no slave to train, I'll just have to use my little brother. Do you remember when you were younger and I used to strip you and flog you? I suppose you don't want any more of that. Or maybe you do. You act as though you'd suit a slave's life more than a freeman's.'

'I'm too old for you to do that to me. Father wouldn't allow it.'

'That's where you're wrong. Don't think I don't know you used to complain to him about my treatment of you. He took me to one side years ago and told me just how far I could go. "Dorian needs a firm hand," he said. "It will do him good to know how a whip feels across his back, just like it did you good when I found it necessary to whip you."'

Dorian looked at Carlos. This was the first he'd heard of this. Carlos realised he'd let something slip, but it was too late to retract it.

'Yes, Father used to whip me. If I did the slightest thing wrong, he would make me strip naked and stand for hours at a time, thinking about my error and what was about to happen to me. He'd even tell the house slaves to come and watch, sometimes. I suppose he felt they would see this as the act of a fair and just master: to flog his own son in front of them. I was never chained or tied. He made me stand still while he put stripes across my back and my arse. If I tried to move away, I got extra strokes. He always said that a freeman had to learn to take it and shouldn't need to be bound to a post. I spared you that at least. Father could never bring himself to do the same to you. He probably saw how soft you were and didn't relish hearing you cry out – that was something I never did. He told me to be fair with you, but firm. He said it was an elder brother's place to discipline the younger one. The only thing he made me promise was not to mark you.'

So, their father had known about Carlos's treatment of Dorian. Dorian had complained once or twice and his father had brushed over the matter. Carlos was a good lad, he'd said. Dorian should listen to his advice and not whinge when Carlos found it necessary to correct him. Dorian assumed his father thought the complaints were exaggerated. Now it was evident he considered it character-building for Dorian to have to endure these humiliations.

'I'm too old for that now,' Dorian repeated. He was stopped from speaking further by the arrival of a messenger. He had been running to catch up with them and was out of breath. He collapsed at the waist, gulping in air, his hands against his knees for support.

'What do you want?' Carlos enquired coldly.

'Carlos and Dorian, guests of Anton?' the messenger asked.

Carlos nodded curtly and was given a folded piece of paper. On it was a note from Anton. It read:

Your father would not thank me should he find I have allowed you to spend your money on an inferior slave. The slave you wanted has been sold to another. I must warn you against any ideas you might have of buying somebody else who has not the approval of either myself or your father. Do not be disappointed: there will be other times and other slaves.

Carlos spat out an expletive and, screwing the note into a ball, cast it into the gutter and continued on his way. Dorian, still unaware of its contents, picked it up and read as he walked.

'You'll have to practise your cruelty on your village friends,' he said.

They were walking down an alley. Further up, where it met the street, people passed and sometimes glanced towards them.

Carlos stopped and stood in front of his brother, blocking the way.

'I don't like that tone, boy. Perhaps I'll teach you a lesson right now.'

Surely not here, not now, thought Dorian. Barely fifty feet away, there were slaves being led to their new homes by their owners. The town was heaving with people. Was he to be degraded here?

'Strip,' Carlos commanded. Dorian didn't move.

Carlos flushed with anger. 'I won't be disobeyed,' he shouted. 'I ordered you to strip. Come on! I want you naked. Now!'

'But . . .'

Dorian realised it was going to be hopeless to protest. Carlos was aroused and, as ever, he was going to take it out on the person nearest to him. That person happened to be Dorian. He could bear it, Dorian told himself. If anybody saw them, they would assume he was a slave Carlos had just bought. They would pay no attention and probably not even register what he looked like.

He was wearing a light tunic and, underneath it, a loincloth. He pulled the tunic over his head and stood before his brother, bare-chested. Carlos looked at him approvingly.

'You always did have a nice body, boy. But I believe I told you to strip naked. I don't see you naked.'

Dorian complied. To his surprise, this felt natural. His cock was growing, try as he might to remain soft.

Carlos reached towards it and coaxed it into rigidity.

'I can see you like this treatment. Maybe I should have sold you and made some money for myself.' Then he barked out. 'Get down on your knees.'

Dorian did so. Carlos stood very near to him. His groin was almost in his brother's face. He lifted his own tunic and pulled down his underwear. His dick was close to Dorian's mouth. Instinctively Dorian opened his lips ready to take it. Carlos seemed pleased with this. He brushed Dorian's lips with the tip of his shaft. The other waited.

Very slowly, Carlos allowed his penis to enter Dorian's mouth. The first part was easy enough, but as he pushed forward Dorian began to gag.

'You're going to take all of it,' Carlos said and pushed further down into Dorian's throat. Dorian tried to resist the temptation to pull away.

'Suck,' Carlos ordered. 'Suck my cock like the slave you are. Come on, I want to feel your lips round my rod.'

Dorian moved his mouth up and down the organ, sucking in as much as he could and trying not to let his teeth graze the sides of Carlos's cock. Carlos moved his hips slowly in and out, savouring the sensation. Dorian's own cock jerked between his legs – it was as though it didn't belong to him.

Carlos manipulated the back of Dorian's head to give more thrust. He moved faster and harder, ignoring the other's splutterings. Dorian could taste the salt and sweat of his brother's groin. His face met coarse pubic hair before it was pulled away each time. Despite the fact that he hated this arrogance and cruelty, Dorian had to admit, only to himself, Carlos was right. This was what he wanted. He was fully aroused.

Before he could reach a climax, Carlos pulled his cock out of Dorian's mouth. The boy sat back on his haunches, waiting to see what was going to happen next.

'I'm not going to beat you,' Carlos said. 'Not this time. But you haven't had enough yet. Stand up and face the wall. Put both your hands above your head and present your arse to me.'

'You're going to fuck me?'

This was something he'd never done before. It meant he really did regard his brother as a slave. Dorian felt a thrill at the prospect of being buggered by his own cruel, handsome, so-called brother.

'Yes, I'm going to fuck you. I'm going to come inside my

little brother's arsehole. I'm going to do it here, where everybody can see. Prepare yourself.'

A tall, slim man was walking towards them. He was bare-chested but for a sash which covered one side of his body. His chest was a mass of thick, black hair. He had a dignified, rather sad face. He must have been about thirty. He stopped and stood a little way off.

'I don't remember that one,' he said, referring to Dorian. 'He must have cost a packet.'

'He's my brother,' Carlos replied. Dorian's emotions collapsed. He might at least have been spared that. Had Carlos pretended he was a slave who had just been bought, the man would have been none the wiser.

'Is he?' the man said. 'May I have a look?'

Dorian had already turned to the wall and was glad his face was hidden. However, Carlos was not going to leave him with any dignity.

'Show the man your body. He wants to look at you.'

Dorian obeyed.

'Keep your hands above your head,' Carlos ordered. Then, turning to the stranger, he said, 'He's all yours, friend. Help yourself.'

The man approached Dorian and stroked the boy's face. Dorian remained subordinate, his eyes cast downward and his hands on his head. His cock was demanding attention. It only added to the utter helplessness of Dorian's situation, jumping slightly of its own accord.

The man came very close. He pressed the length of his body against Dorian's. Dorian used the opportunity to thrust forward with his groin. The movement was slight, but it was enough to feel the man's erection, separated from his own hard-on only by a few layers of thin cloth. This was the only way he had of indicating that he was a freeman with the same rights the man himself had. He was doing this because he wanted to.

The stranger put his finger into Dorian's mouth and used it to prise his teeth apart. Dorian, obeying this unspoken command, opened his mouth. The man pressed his lips against the other's and forced his tongue inside. Dorian let himself be kissed and allowed the man's hands to stroke his naked sides, down towards his cock and his arse. The man pulled away suddenly, panting slightly. Dorian steadied himself and waited.

'He's your brother, you said?'

Carlos nodded.

'Why do you use him like a slave?'

'Why not?'

'You, boy!'

The man was talking to Dorian, who dared not meet the inquisitive look; Carlos would punish him for it. He stirred his feet slightly to acknowledge that he'd heard.

'Why do you let your brother treat you like this? Do you want to be a slave?'

Dorian looked quickly across at Carlos to see whether he had permission to respond. Carlos merely laughed.

'Go on, little brother, answer our friend. Why do you let me treat you like this? Is it because you know it's good for you? Or perhaps this gentleman's right. Perhaps you are of a slave mentality. Your cock certainly seems to respond to my commands.'

'I don't know,' was all Dorian could say. Carlos slapped him lightly across the face.

'Manners,' he snarled. 'You don't know – what?'

'Sir,' Dorian said. 'I don't know, sir.'

'He's very beautiful,' the man continued. 'What can he do with his tongue?'

'Find out if you want. I don't mind being the voyeur for a while. Just don't allow him to come, that's all.'

The man pulled the sash away from his chest and stood before Dorian once more. He ordered the boy to kneel. Dorian did so, ready to take this cock as he had done his brother's. Instead the man turned his back to him and, after pulling away his own underwear, he presented Dorian with his arse.

He had soon pulled the buttocks apart and pushed his hole

against Dorian's lips. His arse was sweaty and Dorian could discern the musky smell which he loved so much. He knew what to do. He reached his tongue towards the puckered skin and began to lick into the forest of hair that surrounded it. Soon the taste of it was in his mouth and he relished every bit of it.

He pushed harder with his tongue; he was inside another's anus, licking round the inside of the shit–hole. The man pushed back and forth against his face. Dorian could tell he was jerking himself off.

Carlos was presumably still watching them. Dorian couldn't see anything but the man's arse close against his own face. His tongue was becoming sore; the acids from the man's body burned in his mouth. He licked across the delicious hole like a cat savouring the last drops of milk on a saucer. The man turned abruptly, shoving his cock into Dorian's face. Dorian tried to take it in his mouth but the stranger used it to slap him away. He pushed Dorian further downwards.

'My balls, boy, lick my balls.'

They were magnificent. Large and, like the rest of his body, covered in hair. Dorian willingly took them into his mouth and coaxed them gently around with his tongue.

The man continued to masturbate furiously. Dorian risked letting go of the testicles for a second or two while he kissed the large, uncircumcised cock. Then he returned to the sack. He licked round it and under it, kissing parts of the skin, under the scrotum and deep into the pubic hair surrounding the man's genitals. Then he took the balls in his mouth once again.

Seconds later he was almost blinded by creamy white semen splashing across his face. The man exhaled deeply and rubbed the come into Dorian's skin. Dorian kissed the proffered hand as he did this. The smell on the man's fingers mingled with the smell of the come on Dorian's face. He lowered his head respectfully. The man pushed him away and began to pull his underwear back into position.

'Are you going to sell him?' he asked Carlos.

'He's not a slave. He's family. No, I'm not going to sell him. I wouldn't be able to even if I wanted to. I'm going to fuck him though. You're welcome to stay while I do.'

Dorian was told to lie on his back and to raise his legs in the air, displaying his arsehole. His brother stripped naked and stood above stroking himself. He had a sheath in his hand which he pulled over his organ before kneeling in between the open legs. The man sat facing Carlos. He slowly rested Dorian's head on his lap. He held the boy's shoulders down, gently but firmly. Carlos pushed with his cock at Dorian's hole. Dorian took deep breaths, awaiting the sudden surge of pain and pleasure he knew was due at any second.

It hurt a lot, but within a few seconds, Dorian's guts adjusted to the huge penis inside him and he was able to thrust in rhythm with it. Carlos leaned over the prone body and their chests met. His face was inches from his brother's. Dorian dared to kiss him. To his surprise Carlos responded.

'Little brother,' he kept saying. 'My little brother . . .'

Dorian felt Carlos filling his inside. He felt complete; he didn't want Carlos to withdraw. Each time he pulled out, Dorian wanted only for him to push back in again. When he did, Dorian felt a warmth which started in his bowels and rose from his chest into his very heart.

Yes, he wanted this; he wanted Carlos to fuck him and to abuse him. He was as good as his brother's slave, even though Carlos had no legal rights over him.

The stranger watched this intently. Dorian was able to use the man's lap as a cushion for his head. He could still smell his juices – they were now dry on his face but still as potent. The man dared to touch Carlos's shoulder and run his hand down his back. Carlos pushed this hand away angrily.

'I'm not for you to have. Keep your hands for this slave-boy brother of mine or on your own body. Leave me alone.'

Dorian tried to kiss Carlos again, but some sort of spell had been broken and Carlos spat into his face. He did so again and again. As his saliva ran down Dorian's cheeks like tears, Carlos came inside him, filling the sheath with his thick, creamy come. Dorian desperately wanted Carlos to kiss him but knew he wouldn't. Carlos lay on top, panting slightly. Then he pulled himself out of his brother's arse, tossed the sheath into the roadside and ordered Dorian to get up.

'Get dressed. We have to go.'

The man rose at the same time and looked at Dorian intently. Dorian avoided his gaze. He knew the meaning in that look. Their companion wanted to know who they were. He wanted to use Dorian again. Dorian wouldn't have wanted to refuse him, but the emotions his brother had stirred inside him were all he could cope with at that moment. He dressed himself, contemplating the unlikely possibility of Carlos changing his attitude towards him. Could the past half-hour be treated as some sort of role-play, as a game?

'Come on, Dorian,' Carlos said. 'We need to get back to Anton's house.' He nodded at the stranger and strode off down the alley. Dorian followed him, not daring to look back.

Rock

The auctioneer's assistant was in his early twenties. He had that burly, bluff character I always associated with country people. His cheerful face showed no malice towards me: he regarded me as he might a cow or a horse.

He stroked my head briefly, twice. Then he slapped me lightly on the backside while pressing down on my shoulder. I stooped – this seemed to be what was required. As soon as my back was bent he placed his hand firmly upon it and pushed me further until I was kneeling on all fours. None of this was done with any hint of superiority or command. It was simply his job to train me.

When I was in the required position, he patted me on the head again and murmured, 'Good boy, good boy.'

I wondered why he hadn't just told me that I was going to have to crawl towards my new master.

He had not released me from my chains and it was difficult to follow him, even though he walked slowly, only occasionally allowing me to overtake him in order that he might give me a swipe across my arse with a light cane. These corrections didn't hurt. They were merely prodding me, urging me to move faster, or in this direction or that.

I felt how I imagined a dog must. Everyone who is part of the world above your head is superior to you. You see only their ankles and feet. Once or twice, one of these lordly beings might stoop to pat you or to stroke your back. (Or, in my case, to run a hand over my cock and balls or to stick a finger into my hole.) The person who leads you also controls you absolutely. He decides who is allowed to touch you and how fast you must go, regardless of the encumbrances he himself has placed around your body. You try your best to anticipate his wishes. You keep close to his ankles. If you please him, you will be petted. If you do not, you will be hit.

The only time the boy acknowledged we shared a language – acknowledged it was even possible to speak to me rather than treat me like a dumb animal – was once when we approached a piece of rough ground with sharp stones strewn over it.

'Go slowly and carefully,' he said. 'The gentleman who's bought you will blame me if you are delivered to him with damaged skin on your knees.'

I didn't want to get the lad into trouble. I held no malice towards him. He was good-hearted and very much of a type I'd seen often before, usually in the kitchens or gardens of my master's house. The fact that he didn't see me as a human being was just a widely held attitude towards slaves which he'd grown up with. He'd been taught the way of things and had learnt his lessons well. In the world of the freemen, he was probably quite low ranking and might even have suffered the odd whipping or caning himself.

Even out of the centre, the town was crowded. I was only one of many slaves. They were either like me – being delivered by boys – or, more frequently, they were slaves already in the charge of their new masters. They were shown off like trophies to their owners' friends and neighbours.

Although the assistant who had control of me was not my owner, he seemed pleased when people assumed him to be. He was complimented on his good taste several times.

'He's got a nice arse, I wouldn't mind being the man who owns that.'

'Your master's going to have his cock down your throat before you can take a breath in.' (This said to me with a nod and wink to the boy – 'my master'.)

Once he intervened on my behalf:

'Let me feel his dick.'

Without waiting for permission, the man reached for my cock from behind and felt up and down its length. It was still hard, of course. The man began to masturbate me. I had to pull away or else give in to my physical need and shoot my load.

The boy saw the danger and came to my rescue.

'He's not your property. He's been bought by someone. Leave him alone.'

The man desisted reluctantly. My penis was aching for such attention. No doubt I would be allowed to come soon enough. The assistant kicked me gently on my backside to start me crawling again. He went ahead, leaving me to suffer the attentions of the crowd as before.

Presently, we came to a large house. The boy reached inside his satchel and brought out a length of leather with a buckle. This was attached to a chain, on the end of which was a ring. Deftly, he forced the leather into my mouth, pushing my tongue back and my teeth slightly apart. He buckled it at the back of my head and, taking the chain and ring, tethered me to a peg which had been driven into the ground for that purpose.

Then he took my wrists and, roughly positioning them behind my back, bound me tightly. He pushed me into an upright kneeling position with my groin forced forward and my head back.

He couldn't resist running his hand over my cock and balls, but only briefly. Then he instructed me verbally for the second time.

'This is how your new owner will first see you. Make sure you match up to his expectations. He'll come to claim you when he's ready.'

He disappeared inside the building but was out again in a few moments. No doubt he had told whoever was inside that their new purchase had been delivered and was awaiting them.

As he gave me one last look, I could read lust in his face. No doubt he would take this out on some minor slave belonging to either the auctioneer or another official.

He left me, bound again, gagged and with the beginnings of tears springing into my eyes.

I had been placed in an obscene position. My legs were wide apart so passers-by could see my cock more easily – gorged and hungry, thrusting forward from my pubic hair. It seemed worse that I had to maintain my posture without being restrained into it. My compliance somehow underlined that I had accepted my position as nothing more than a piece of property belonging to some other man.

The passers-by didn't spare me. I was pointed at, laughed at and, more than a few times, told what my new master would be likely to do to this body, so on display. I bit into my gag and waited, my heart thumping.

It was some hour and a half before I heard footsteps approaching the door of the house. This was it; I was about to meet the man who would, from now on, be in charge of my destiny. The man who would have absolute power over me. He might be brutal or kind, old or young, ugly or beautiful.

Strangely, thoughts of Theo kept flashing into my head. I wondered whether he was tied up outside somebody else's house. I wondered whether his muscular, hairy body was on display like mine and I wondered if he would be content with his lot. Even now, I hoped against hope we had been bought by the same person. He might be already inside, waiting for me.

The heavy oak door of the building was opened and I bowed my head. I wasn't sure whether this was the thing to do, but it would be unlikely I would be punished for it – as I probably would be if I looked my new owner straight in the eye.

A hand reached under my chin and gently lifted my face upwards.

I would have gasped had it not been for the gag in my mouth.

Looking at me was my old master, Anton.

'Rest now. You will soon be instructed in what will happen to you.'

I had been taken inside the house. My arms had been freed and I had been ungagged. Anton had washed me with his own hands using a cloth and a bowl of warm, scented water. He had applied oil to my body, massaging it into my shoulder blades, my pectorals and my stomach. He put more than was necessary on to my cock, gently sliding his hand along it. I managed not to allow the feeling to mount to orgasm. He sat back and looked at me for a moment or two.

'You're very lovely to look at. Let me see you relieve your desire.'

I was grateful for two reasons. The first, and most urgent, was my need to empty my aching balls. The second was that this meant I would not be used too much that night. A slave who was allowed to come would usually be given enough time to rest before having to get hard again.

I stood before him and jerked myself off: slowly at first, but it didn't take long before I was pulling harder and harder. My knees gave way slightly as the spunk began to force itself up, right from the base of my organ. I could feel every bit of it pulsating from my balls: up my cock and out like a fountain on to the floorboards in front of me. My legs were made weak by it; my stomach collapsed inward and my face must have contorted. I gasped and panted as I squeezed the last drop of semen out of my body. Then I tried to regain some control. I stood with my legs slightly apart and my hands hanging loosely by my sides. Anton smiled at me.

'You needed that, I can see. Now I expect you're curious to know what has happened and why I am here.'

I nodded respectfully.

'I am no longer your owner, but I have been given charge of you until such time as he arrives. It was my agent who made the crucial bid for you but not with my own money. It was strange to be given this responsibility for, as you're aware, the money I paid for you on behalf of another will mostly come back to me as your previous owner. However, the man who entrusted me with your purchase cares little for how much he spends. He was most particular you were to be his property. Other than that I don't yet know, apart from being able to tell you this man is fair and just and I have known him for some years. It was his son who flogged you the other day and his other son who took quite an interest in you at that time. Soon he will send for you in order to determine whether his money has been well spent. It's not for me to say, but I would guess you are going to be given as a present to one or the other of his sons.'

Five

Justin waited patiently by the man who had taken him. The formalities of payment over, he was now the property of some unknown freeman, or so he assumed. He was taken to a small tavern, not far away from the market and there left outside, untethered but still in chains, while his minder refreshed himself.

Some customers at another table cast approving looks at him.

'I don't usually go for fair-haired men, but that's a beauty,' said one.

'He has good skin colour, that's why,' returned another. 'It sets off the green of his eyes. Look, let me show you . . .'

He was about to approach Justin in order to demonstrate his point. Before he could do so, Justin's escort reappeared. Surprisingly, he had not one, but two glasses of warm beer in his hands. One of these he'd already drunk from; the other he set down.

'Drink,' was all he said.

Justin grasped the beer and gulped it down far too quickly. The man placed a hand on his arm.

'I don't want to have to carry you. Take it slowly.'

'Thank you, Master,' Justin replied.

The man smiled. He was rough, avuncular and he had a strange accent. His age was about forty, but his large body was by no means out of condition. Justin had assumed him to be a soldier of some sort. He wore a leather jerkin and rough canvas breeches. His beard was clipped close to his skin, but the effect of this was at odds with his weather-beaten face. So far he had shown little interest in Justin's naked body. Even now, he cast only a fleeting glance in his charge's direction.

'I'm not your master,' he said. 'I can't say more until we are well away from this damned place. Drink, but slowly. It will do you good.'

Justin didn't need telling twice. He savoured the unfamiliar taste of the beer while his companion drank his own in silence.

When they had finished, the man indicated for Justin to follow him. He led him through numerous backstreets to the edges of the town. Once they were out of sight of any passers-by, the man took a key and unlocked Justin's chains. He reached inside a bag which he had slung over one shoulder, producing from it a pair of breeches like his own and a cotton shirt.

'Put these on,' he grunted. 'Let's have you looking like a human being, shall we?'

Justin still didn't dare query any of this. He was glad enough of the clothes and even more at having been rid of his fetters – they were left where they had fallen. As soon as he was dressed his companion simply turned and carried on his way, apparently careless of whether Justin followed or not. Clothed and unchained, Justin considered making a run for it, but he was too curious. He caught up with the man and they walked swiftly in the direction of the sea.

Once at the beach, the man stopped again. He sat down on a piece of driftwood and lit a pipe. Justin stood for a moment, uncertain of what to do. Then he sat down beside the man.

'Where are we going?' he asked.

'It will be explained in time,' was the reply. 'Don't worry, I think we can assure you that we won't need chains on your arms or legs to keep you with us.'

He took a draw on the evil-smelling pipe. 'We have to wait here. It will be a while, I should think.'

'You said you weren't my master,' Justin began. 'Is my master to take me on from here? Is it him we're waiting for?'

'You've been too long a slave, boy. Why do you think I've given you clothing and unchained you?'

He said this without looking at Justin. He was smoking and staring out to sea. His comments seemed like casual conversation. Hope began to rise in Justin's mind, only to be supplanted by bitter cynicism.

'I've never heard of a slave being given clothing unless it was there to be torn off him again. Clothing for us is like wrapping on a parcel. You'll have me naked again soon enough.'

'If I were one of them, I'd whip you for that remark.'

The man turned to look at Justin. His grey eyes had something of amusement in them. His voice betrayed no reprimand. 'Luckily for you, I'm not one of them. I have no interest in your body, son. You can keep your cock for those who want it.'

'Who are you? Who's bought me? I don't understand.'

The man pointed out to sea. A vessel was just visible on the horizon.

'Here she comes now. Where are the others, I wonder?'

He lapsed back into silence, smoking his pipe and ignoring Justin.

The ship slowly approached the beach.

Rock

Anton preceded me into the room. It was bare of furniture, save for a throne-like seat at one end. The ceilings were high and the archways which let in the light also admitted a cooling breeze. It was late evening.

Anton led me into the centre of this space and made me stand, indicating that I should bow my head. I had already observed the occupant of the room. He was, maybe, fifty-six or fifty-seven. He had the bearing of a soldier. His hair was iron grey and he wore a neat, trimmed beard but had no moustache. His eyes were a cold green colour, but they didn't give him a stern or frightening appearance; rather, he seemed sad and reflective. His figure was trim, maybe even skinny, but his open shirt showed a chest which had stood up to the impairments of time. The hair here was mostly black, flecked with grey here and there. No doubt when he was younger it had been soft and downy; now it was grizzled and wiry. He wore a short tunic which showed his legs. A much younger man would have been proud to own them.

He rose from the seat and greeted Anton with a light kiss on each cheek.

'Let's see what you have brought me,' he said. His voice was deep and resonant. I decided, already, that I liked him.

He approached me and walked around my body, looking carefully over my flesh. The examination was routine: he put his fingers inside my mouth and prised it open, peering inside to check my teeth and tongue. He ran his hand through my hair and grunted approvingly. He prodded and patted my buttocks, separating them to check my arsehole. His finger went in there as well, pushing upwards and probing inside me. I tried to remain still and he seemed pleased with the feel of me.

He then squatted in front of my genitals. Lifting my penis, he gently squeezed my sack and, with his other hand, stroked my pubes. He massaged my cock into life and even kissed the end of it, more, I suspected, to check the taste of my body fluids than to give me any pleasure. He paid particular attention to each of my nipples, making sure they were sensitive and seeing how much his finger and thumb could make me squirm. Again I tried to remain still, but he appeared to be gratified when I hissed in a sharp breath as the sensation stabbed across my chest.

'He's quite a lad,' he said. 'And cheap too – or, at least, cheap enough to afford. Not, I suspect, a price anywhere near the affordability of my sons' pockets.'

Anton laughed.

'They couldn't go anywhere near the asking price. And I sent them word they were to hold on to their money. I took the liberty of suggesting to them you would need to give your permission should they decide to buy a different slave: one that hadn't been vetted by me or your good self. When they arrive at my house, they will find instructions for them to come to this address.'

'They don't suspect anything then? That's good. I want this young man to be a surprise for them.'

He turned to me.

'You are, as you have no doubt been told, a gift for my two

sons. I trust you are as obedient as I have been led to believe by my friend here. If you fail in your duties or I hear any sort of complaint about your behaviour, you will be flogged. You already know that my eldest son is particularly good with a whip. It will be him who is given the job of reminding you of your position should it be necessary. Do I make myself clear?'

'Yes, Master,' I mumbled.

'On the other hand, if you perform well and behave yourself, you will have a relatively easy time. My youngest son is, I am told, fond of you. He will look after you and care for you. You will be, shall we say, his pet.'

He paused, reflecting on this description.

'Yes,' he continued. 'A pet is what you will be. I expect you to become almost part of the family but never so much that you get above yourself. I will not have you mistreated or cruelly used, but your place will not be at my table, but under it. You do understand, I hope?'

'I understand, sir,' I said.

He turned then to Anton.

'I have a fancy – this is rather sentimental of me – I would like him gift-wrapped. Would you be able to see to it for me? I want to present him to my boys after supper. Will that give you enough time?'

Anton laughed again. He seemed to be greatly pleased by his friend's reaction to me.

'I'll have Marvin do it straight away. On condition I have an invitation to dinner and am able to see them opening him.'

Marvin was summoned and I was taken to another room. As was usual with Marvin, he made no comment on what he had been told, but merely set about obeying his orders, efficiently and briskly.

He made me stand with my hands by my sides. He regarded me for a moment or two. I could tell he was wondering how best I should be presented. I might as well have been a rather oddly shaped toy he had been told to parcel up.

He decided on bandages first of all. I was going to be restrained in the way the Ancient Egyptians swathed their dead. He held the coarse cloth at my navel and began to pull it tightly around my middle. When it held, he quickly covered my midriff in the stuff. My arms were pinioned by it and my body squeezed tight. Before long, he had covered me up to my nipples. Here the length of bandage ran out and he produced a second piece.

This was used to cover my upper chest, up to my shoulders. He left my face for later, fixing the loose end of bandage with a pin just by my throat.

Next he attended to my legs. He began at my ankles and wrapped me just up to my groin. When this stage was complete, I was mummified apart from my head and my sexual organs.

I felt more naked then than I had ever felt when I was stripped. The bandages around the rest of my body accentuated the coolness of the air playing around my cock and balls. An observer would have his attention drawn to my genitalia far more readily than had I been a nude body presented for his inspection.

Marvin might have known this, or he might simply have been saving my prick till last. He did my face next. My eyes were covered and then my forehead, my hair, under my chin and across my mouth. Thankfully, he was careful to leave my nostrils exposed.

I was cocooned in tight material, completely unable to move my limbs. Strangely, it felt safe and almost comfortable.

Marvin began fingering my cock. He may have needed it to be erect so as to give me room to be hard. Whatever the case, he rubbed at me until I began to undulate gently as much as I was able to.

This signalled to him the danger of my shooting my spunk before I was to be allowed. My sexual organs were swiftly bound and the material fixed somewhere next to the small of my back.

From inside my soft prison, I could make out the rustling of paper. Marvin's hands supported me as I was laid face upward upon it. I sensed the paper being tucked around me. After making some sort of slit near my nose, enough for me to breathe easily, he secured the whole thing with string, pulling it tight and tying knots at various points.

I was then placed inside a coffin-like crate. The lid was closed upon me and I was left alone with my thoughts.

I desperately wanted to come.

Six

———

Dinner was a subdued affair. The two boys were still disappointed at not having achieved their aim of buying Rock for themselves. Carlos was less despondent than his brother: he would have enough bodies to do with as he pleased, but he still felt cheated of his prey.

Dorian was silent throughout the meal. He had wanted the slave, of course he had, but it was more than that. He was worried about where Rock might have been taken and who might now be his master. He kept telling himself that the chances of his lover having been bought by a considerate, reasonable owner were many and extremely likely. On the other hand, it was eminently possible that Rock might, even now, be suffering gross maltreatment at the hands of one such as Carlos or even worse.

He had been pleased when, on returning to Anton's house, they had received news of their father. They had hurried to the address they'd been given and been warmly welcomed by their indulgent parent. Their father seemed overtly interested in the market and what had transpired there. Carlos was happy enough to provide him with the details and Dorian only had to nod occasionally when asked, 'Is that so?' or similar, unimportant questions.

Anton, he thought, was unusually cheerful. Perhaps it was because of his success in selling his boys. This end of the day found him a richer man than when he had awoken. Even so, Dorian knew he had been very fond of the men he owned and it was strange that he didn't seem to be very worried about what had happened to them.

'There's a register,' he had said at one point. 'I can find out where they've gone when I need to. As a matter of fact, I believe Theo and Justin have both managed to find very suitable homes indeed. The other one – well, I expect he's all right.'

Although their father had hired staff for his visit, it was Anton's only remaining slave who served them. Dorian caught him smirking at his master's allusion to Rock. He wanted to reprimand him for it, but he couldn't muster the energy. He planned to sneak off once the meal was over and see if he could find out more information on Rock's fate. He didn't quite know what he would do if it proved to be bad news, but he wanted to know. He prayed Anton's words were true and he was worrying unnecessarily.

Eventually, drinks were served. Dorian refused his and was about to excuse himself. His father stopped him.

'My two sons, come here. I have something of a surprise for you.'

He seemed almost boyish. He was barely concealing a grin and kept glancing at Anton and rubbing his hands. Dorian felt a great warmth for him. He evidently realised how disappointed they were and had bought them some trifle to make up for it. He determined to be thrilled with whatever it was, though he suspected it would be no more useful than the hideous scarf he had been presented with before he left for Illyria.

They went and stood by him. He gave Marvin a nod and the slave left the room to get the present.

'You will be coming home soon,' their father said. 'I wanted you to know how pleased I am with your progress during your time away and how gratified I am that my old friend speaks so well of you. You've been a credit to me.'

He turned to Dorian. 'I know you were set on having a slave of your own. I'm sorry your meagre allowance didn't provide you with the funds to purchase the one you wanted. I would not, however, have been pleased if you'd squandered your money on some inferior specimen. I want my sons to have the best when they are able to afford it.'

'I understand that,' Dorian said. 'Please don't think I'm ungrateful. I usually have more than enough money for my needs.'

'Apart from when you fall in love with some captive Adonis,' Carlos interjected. 'He was practically drooling, Father. It's just as well he couldn't afford to buy him. He would have halved the value of the man in less than a month.'

'In love?' Their father looked concerned. 'Is this true, Dorian?'

Dorian was angry with his brother, but not so much that his emotions couldn't be checked.

'What's wrong with that? Yes, I was in love with him. He may not be a freeman and I didn't intend to treat him like one. But I prefer to take a man to my bed to share our bodies together rather than have him hate me for my cruelty.'

Carlos sneered and looked the other way. The older man banged the table with his fist.

'Enough of this bickering. I won't have it. I was going to –'

He was interrupted by a knock at the door. Marvin entered the room and asked whether they were ready.

'A moment. I need to talk to my sons for a moment or two. Wait outside with the, er, gift.'

Marvin retreated to join two hired servants outside the door.

'You two are very different from one another,' their father went on. 'I know you have no shared blood between you, but I always hoped you would grow up like real brothers and support each other. It hasn't been the case. You, Carlos, are too ready to criticise and you are not above using your seniority to indulge some of your more unsavoury desires.'

Carlos was about to protest but he was ignored.

'And you, Dorian. You are not one whose natural instincts incline you to the responsibility which goes with your status. You are good at heart, but you are not strong enough. Your two different personalities should complement one another. Indeed they do, but you must stop this squabbling between yourselves. It is for Carlos to protect Dorian and Dorian to respect Carlos. These things are essential if you are to maintain any kind of life together when I am gone.'

The two looked uncomfortable and remained silent. Their father often talked of the time when he would no longer be there. It seemed morbid and premature. He was still fit and, although past the best years allotted to him, he would surely live for a long time.

He read their thoughts. 'I will die – we all must. Before that happens I have the disagreeable thought of old age to look forward to. I say disagreeable, because that's what it will be if you two boys can't be brothers together. If you cannot, you will soon no longer be able to stand each other's company and you will go your separate ways. I can't bear the thought of being without you now. Especially when I contemplate the very real possibility of infirmity. I can feel my body gradually diminishing in its prowess. Who knows what the next twenty years might bring? I want to be sure of my security. I deserve that from you at least.'

Dorian knelt and grasped his father's hand.

'I will always be here for you, Father,' he said. 'Carlos can do as he pleases. I will look after you. You have your security.'

'Apart from the time when I crook my little finger and you come running to me,' Carlos said unkindly. 'You hate me, but you can't resist me. You know that's true. It's time to be honest about it.'

Their father rarely lost his temper. He almost never shouted or even raised his voice. This comment pushed him over the edge of his usual control. He exploded with anger.

'Isn't this what I'm talking about, boy? You're speaking of your brother as though he had the mind of a slave!'

Carlos looked shaken but held his ground. He looked his father in the eye.

'He's not my brother – you said so yourself. And he does have the mind of a slave. Ask him to deny it if he can. At least he's honest.'

Dorian had lowered his head on to his father's lap. His nerves were on edge. He expected his father to ask the question and, Carlos was right, he couldn't deny it. He felt as though he'd let down both himself and his benefactor. Yet, was it his fault? He couldn't help the way he was.

Their father was quiet for a while. When he spoke it was in his usual calm, authoritative voice.

'If what you say is true – and I will not ask as you suggest – if it is true, then it is no disgrace. Some men do have the instincts to serve and some to command. At least I know Dorian will be true to himself and will not counter his natural inclinations with hatred and bitterness.'

He looked Carlos straight in the eye.

'What are your natural inclinations, my son? Do you know? Or are you so frightened of what is in your own heart that you mask it with this venomous exterior? It is not good.' He shook his head sadly. 'Not good at all.'

Carlos spat on the floor. His eyes were fiery with rage.

'I'm leaving. Keep your present. You always favoured him above me. I don't need either of you.'

He stormed out of the room, leaving the door open. Marvin, still waiting on the other side of the door, was knocked aside by his exit.

There was a long silence. Anton was running his finger around the edge of his glass and looking thoughtful. Dorian still had his head buried in his father's lap. His father was looking straight ahead, at the same time patting Dorian's head to comfort him.

Marvin coughed and edged into the room.

'Do you want me to take the box away, sir?' he asked.

Dorian's father pulled himself out of his reverie and attempted a smile.

'No, no,' he said. 'I'll present it to you, Dorian. I still say it will belong to both of you, but I think your brother needs a little more time here in Illyria. If that is acceptable to you, Anton.'

Anton nodded his assent.

'I will be going to stay with relatives for some months. You will travel home alone, Dorian. Or at least – not alone. Bring it in, slave.'

Marvin beckoned to the two other servants who entered behind him carrying a large crate. It was the size of a man and studded with air-holes. Was it possible? Dorian tried to dismiss the thought, but it hovered around the edges of his mind. The crate was placed on the ground in front of him.

'Open it,' his father said. 'I think you will be more pleased than you were with my taste in scarves.'

Dorian obeyed, hardly daring to hope it contained what he supposed it to.

Inside was a mass of paper tied with string. Dorian's heart sank. Presumably it was some statue. It didn't move and there was no obvious sign of breathing.

His mind went over the possibilities as he tore at the paper. If it couldn't breathe, why the air-holes? If it was a living thing, why was it wrapped in paper? Why couldn't he see it moving?

The paper off, a bandaged figure was revealed. It was warm and soft to the touch. Dorian began to cut back the material around the waist. Underneath was real, living skin and hair. A man's ribs, his navel, his abdomen . . .

The rise and fall of breath was discernible now. Dorian cut upward from the stomach to the neck. He knew this chest. He knew those nipples and those pectoral muscles. He wanted to cry out like a child who has been given his favourite doll.

The bandages around the face fell away and Dorian put his arms around Rock who, his hands now free, responded. He was not chastised for this.

They kissed and the older men smiled indulgently.

'I've shown you where there is a bedchamber,' Dorian's father said. 'Take him there. I think you need to lie down for a little while. Tomorrow you can take him home.'

Rock

My mummified state had been curiously comforting. Lying there in the dark, I had felt safe and peaceful. When it had become clear to me what Marvin's intentions were, I had immediately anticipated claustrophobia and guarded myself against it. I told myself I would make my mind a blank: meditate on the colours shifting from blue to purple to black against my closed eyes. This I had done and, despite nagging fears, a voice within me had counselled that I must give myself over to fate. I had no control over what would now happen to me, to my body. I must let events take their course, whether for good or for ill.

Soon my crowded brain cleared and I think I actually fell asleep.

When my coffin-like crate was eventually lifted, I experienced a momentary feeling of panic. I forced myself to dismiss it. My hearing was muffled because of the bandages about my ears, but I heard various doors being opened and closed. Somehow I sensed we did not leave the confines of the house. Presently, I was set down and I steeled myself for imminent unwrapping and whatever else would follow.

I was to be given as a gift: which boy would take precedence over my treatment? Somehow I doubted it would be my lover. More than likely I was about to suffer another beating at the hands of the elder youth.

We waited for what seemed like an age before I was again lifted and, shortly after, set down once more. The lid of the crate was lifted and the paper around my body was torn away. The bandages were cut, causing my body to tingle as the air caressed it. A hand stroked my stomach. It was a caring, gentle hand. I dared to hope it belonged to my lover.

Even when my arms had been freed, I had the sense to keep them by my sides. I didn't know what was expected of me. By now I was sure of who it was pulling the bindings away from my body.

He left freeing my face till last. The material peeled away: I dared to open my eyes and was rewarded by an embrace and then a kiss which was so passionate it made my head spin.

I looked at him with a kind of wonder. He was more handsome than I remembered. His youthful face was lit with pleasure; his sleek, black hair with its one wayward lock gave him the look of a romantic hero from the old legends. My fears faded into the background. Let the other one abuse me as much as he wanted. My pain would be worth suffering if I could be near this beautiful boy. I was in love and I knew it.

My joints were stiff from my confinement. My lover helped me to stand. Rising from the crate was like being born all over again. I was entering a new life just as I had entered the world itself: naked and newly released from the protection and restrictions of the womb.

Other people were in the room. I was vaguely aware of them, but my eyes were fixed on the kind, gentle face of my new master. He held my hands in his, squeezing them as though to confirm his pleasure in beholding his new property.

One of the others spoke to him; it must have been his father. I was to be taken to my lover's bed.

As soon as the door closed behind us, he turned to me and smiled. He still held my hand in his.

'Don't worry,' was all he said.

He led me down long corridors to the bedroom. It was sparse enough, but comfortable and welcoming. A large bed and a small table were the only items of furniture. The light filtered in from a small window, set rather too high up in the wall. The floor was covered in smooth, warm matting. I stood just inside the door, waiting.

Now we were alone we seemed like a shy couple on their wedding night. Neither of us quite knew what was expected or what we should do. He faltered, but it was not for me to make the first move. I guessed he supposed me to regard him as any slave might his master: as a freeman, a privileged oppressor, someone to be resented.

Although I sensed my feelings for him were reciprocated, I was still unsure of how far I might transgress the normal rules which governed our situation. After all, I was no more than a piece of his property.

My instincts told me I was stronger, more sure of myself than he would ever be. I wanted to embrace him again. I wanted to smother him with kisses and pull him down to the bed. There I would slowly undress him, revealing each part of his body as he had mine. When we were naked together, I would make love to him, just as I had wanted to since first I saw him.

We stood facing each other. At the very moment I was about to give way to my impulses, he visibly suppressed his evident passivity and assumed an affected air of authority.

'You are now my slave,' he said, sounding unconvincing. 'You are to obey me. If you do, I will not have to punish you. If you don't, I'll —'

The blood rushed into his cheeks and he lowered his eyes. I waited patiently, knowing this façade would crumble before long. He recovered his composure, jerking the insistent strand of hair from his eyes.

'I'll have to either beat you myself, or give you over to my brother, who is also your master.'

Clearly, he would rather this last statement had not been the case. It was added lamely – almost apologetically. Still I waited. In the silence which followed, the truth of our relationship communicated between us. It was stronger than the words he spoke. I trusted it enough to look him in the eye. Though he was fighting against it, I knew it would overtake him soon enough.

'Don't imagine I will be soft with you,' he went on. 'I may be younger than you and not as hard as my brother, but I can do it, you know.'

This sounded so charmingly untrue that it made me smile. I didn't even try to hide it. He avoided my eyes again and moved behind me so I couldn't see his discomfort.

After what seemed like a long time he said, very quietly, 'You're very beautiful.'

His hand brushed across my shoulder blades and traced a path downward, down between my buttocks and under, stroking my balls. He held me, bringing his body close against mine. I could feel his hot breath on my neck. His free hand toyed with my hair and his lips brushed against my ear.

It was enough. He was either going to acknowledge the reality of what we both felt, or he was going to stumble through some pretence of authority and attempt to punish me. I doubted such punishment would be anything like as bad as I had experienced when Anton owned me.

I eased away and turned to face him. He suddenly seemed frightened: of me? Of his feelings? Of his brother? I didn't know and I didn't care. I grabbed him and kissed him roughly. His body went limp in my arms. I pressed my lips against his until they hurt. He made a vain attempt to keep his mouth closed but not for more than a second or two. His startled eyes stared into mine but they couldn't lie. He wanted me.

I moved him to the bed and pushed him on to it. He lay there, saying nothing, looking at me as though I were the only thing in the world. I spoke for the first time.

'Yes, you own me,' I said. 'You may punish me at the end

of this. You might even give me over to your brother to flog. I don't fear that. He's done it before and I suppose, whatever happens, he will do it again.'

I placed my body over his and began to undo the fastenings on his tunic. His chest was heaving and I could hear his heart thumping. He was compliant enough to lift his body so I could pull the garment off his shoulders. He lay back: half-naked, passive. I brought my face to the side of his and whispered in his ear.

'We have to be true to what we are. Men may make us slaves or masters. We may be punished, ridiculed or scorned, but we know what lies inside our hearts. I will not betray you or use our love for each other against you. I know you don't want us to pretend when we are alone.'

By now we were holding each other as though no difference in our status had ever existed.

'Love?' he said quietly. 'Do you think it's that, too?'

'I know it. I knew it from the first time I saw you. Others may laugh at that, but it's true. What's more, it's strong enough here –' I put my hand over my heart '– to know it must be there in you. What I feel would not exist if it wasn't reflected back. I am a slave, but I'm also a man. In a moment or two we will both be naked. We will both be equal. Don't fight your feelings.'

I knelt upright and shifted down his legs to give me access to the lower part of his tunic. He watched as I pulled it apart. From his expression, I might have supposed him to be as curious to see what lay beneath as I was myself. White cotton covered his sex but the cloth was flimsy enough to see he was hard. I put my hand on his cock and squeezed. He sighed pleasurably and closed his eyes. With one swift moment, I ripped the remaining covering off him.

My mouth closed over his cock. The musky aroma of his sweat, caught in the wonderful bush of black pubic hair, filled my nostrils. I breathed it in as I sucked him. His hips rose and fell gently. His fingers pressed against my head, kneading my scalp like a cat surrendering to its desire for comfort.

My lips eventually found new pleasure with his balls. I licked around them before holding them gently in my mouth. Then I went down further, lifting his legs to give me access to his backside.

His arse was clean and tight. My tongue darted in and out of his hole, into the place where I wanted my cock to be.

When I had had my fill of that pleasure, I moved up his body and sucked on his nipples. He held me against his chest, stroking my hair while I chewed gently at each of the tender peaks.

Presently, he lifted my head up and for a whole minute we gazed into each other's eyes, letting the unspoken contract of our affection sink home in both our hearts. I eased myself up the bed to his face and we kissed again.

'This is wrong,' he said hoarsely. 'We shouldn't be feeling this.'

'I know,' I replied. 'Remember what I said. If you're true to your feelings, it won't matter what others say.'

'I can't let you fuck me,' he said. 'I'm sorry. I can't. People would know.'

'It's all right,' I assured him. 'I don't want anything you can't give freely.'

He still seemed troubled. He turned on to his side and, for a moment or two, was lost in his own thoughts. I let him have the time he needed. To tell the truth, I was as disturbed as he was. The power of emotion was not a luxury I was used to. This love was a wonderful thing, but it could also prove to be the cause of much heartache. I knew that and I did not dismiss the fact lightly.

'What are we going to do?' he said at last.

'Tell me everything you feel,' I answered, trying to sound assured and confident. 'Be honest with me and to yourself. If we know the problems we can guard against them.'

'It's my brother. He's going to be cruel to you, I know it. I don't think I can bear to see him hurting you. He already suspects the truth. If he finds out we're together – together in this way – he'll take it out on you. He'll try and humiliate me through his power over you.'

I waited before replying, letting the pause add weight to my words.

'I am a slave. I have been a slave for many years. I'm used to harsh treatment. Your brother is going to whip me and make me suffer in all sorts of ways. I know. If such treatment means I can be near to you, I will take it gladly.'

For an hour we held each other. Neither of us needed more from that first meeting of our bodies. When he decided it was time for us to go back to the outside world, he seemed more assured. It was strange, but his admission of love for me had made him stronger, more in control. I was happy to be his slave and he seemed more at ease with being my owner. I would return with him to his home; his brother would not follow for some time. Till then we would be safe together and would work out the parameters of our relationship.

What had passed between us was not to be referred to for a long time to come. I knew I would have to subjugate myself to his authority. Not only in the presence of others; it was important for him that it should be so in our private life together. The time would come when this might change, but it was for him to say when that time had come.

Seven

There was a shallow pool at the back of his father's house in which Dorian bathed when the weather was hot. It was one of his favourite places: cool and welcoming, surrounded by plants and visited by exotic birds. The water came to about the height of his chest. It was deep enough to wallow in, but not so deep he had to make any effort to keep his head above it. Other members of his father's household tended not to use the pool and Dorian sometimes fancied it to be his own private place where he could go to think and unwind after the day's studies. His brother seldom bothered to go anywhere near it. He always said lounging around water was a thing women do.

In any case, Dorian hadn't seen Carlos for a month or so. On their father's advice, the elder son had stayed in Illyria.

In those first few weeks when they were alone together, Rock rarely left his young master's side. He was brought to the pool each day and there he slowly and lovingly washed Dorian's back for him, kissing various parts of the boy's skin as he passed his strong hands over him.

Then he would gradually begin to massage his shoulders. Dorian allowed the muscles to relax as Rock kneaded into his flesh – down his spine, vertebra by vertebra. He often succumbed to the feeling of drowsiness which would overtake him. When this happened, Rock gently lifted him out of the water and laid him on his stomach, by the pool's edge. With his fingers, he would work his way up Dorian's legs and on to his buttocks.

Dorian was usually covered round his waist. He would feel Rock reach inside the wet cloth, gently probing the crack between his buttocks and lightly brushing the skin around his arsehole.

Dorian especially loved Rock's strong hands rubbing down the sides of his torso. The physical closeness made him feel safe and secure.

The muscles of his upper back were often knotted from the strains of the day. The heels of Rock's palms would soon work the tension away and to do this, Rock had to sit astride him. Close against his buttocks, Dorian felt his slave's hard meat nestling between those fabulous legs. The hot flesh pressed pleasantly into his body: more so as the rhythm of the massage built up.

After having his fill of this, Dorian motioned for Rock to move to allow him to turn onto his back. This done, Rock took a position astride him once more. With their two cocks now so close, Rock massaged the front of Dorian's chest. Then he would use his mouth to stimulate each sensitive nipple.

From there he licked and kissed down Dorian's stomach almost as far as his groin. His thumbs entered at either side of his owner's balls. Dorian squirmed with pleasure as he was stimulated round the sides of his testicles. If he could take this, he would allow it to go on. If it became too much, he would dive into the pool to cool off and take away some of the lust which had built up.

However, it was not unusual for him to be taken over completely. When this happened, he loosened the cloth around his waist and his slave would recognise this as permission to take his eager mouth down further. Then Rock would nuzzle into his pubic hair, licking the tightly contracted sack of soft skin which held his balls. Gradually, very gradually, Dorian would feel the tip of his slave's tongue go further up his sexual organs, finally jabbing and licking around his piss-slit.

Then Rock licked all around the head of Dorian's cock, gently and teasingly, before enveloping the whole organ in his mouth and sucking while Dorian groaned with pleasure. After this, Dorian pushed him off and made him take a position on all fours, with his head flat to the ground and his arse – beautiful and rounded, firm and muscular – raised invitingly, ready to be invaded.

Dorian greased Rock gently and the slave moaned quietly as a finger entered his guts. When the arsehole was ready, Dorian pulled a sheath over his throbbing organ and pushed himself between the manly thighs.

Dorian liked to press himself against Rock before he entered him. This seemed to drive the slave to distraction. He would begin thrusting himself backward urgently – demanding to have his shit-hole plugged by his young master's meat. Dorian then entered him, relishing the gasp as he did so. He felt Rock's arse muscles tighten along the length of his cock, sucking it into his insides.

He let Rock's clenched muscles pull and squeeze around his dick before he began fucking him. Soon he was thrusting furiously, Rock responding by moving his body back against Dorian's in time with his rhythm.

Before he could come, Dorian collapsed along Rock's back, his lower body still pumping into him, but more slowly than before. Then he reached round and felt Rock's magnificent cock and began to wank him. It wasn't long before they both came: Dorian into Rock's body and Rock spattering thick, creamy white gobs over the ground and Dorian's hand.

Dorian made the slave lick his own semen from his fingers before withdrawing and taking Rock's wonderful body in his arms and plunging his tongue into the waiting mouth. They could stay like that for a long time, holding each other and exploring each other's mouths and faces with their tongues. Then they plunged into the cooling water and, for a time, would be as they had been that first time together: equals and friends rather than master and slave.

Rock slept at the foot of his master's bed, like a pet dog. Dorian knew he would not run away, but he tethered him all the same – with a light metal chain round one of his ankles. This Dorian attached to the heavy iron leg of the bed. He didn't know whether Rock was offended by this treatment. Presumably, he had been made to suffer the indignity of worse fetters.

Once, Dorian had to pass water in the middle of the night.

Rock stirred as soon as Dorian rose from the bed. When it became clear what Dorian was about to do, Rock knelt with his head back and his mouth open, expecting to be used to piss into.

At the time, Dorian didn't want to, but the prospect intrigued and excited him. He let his urine flow into the waiting mouth.

The following night, Dorian made Rock open his mouth for him again and, once more, he let his bladder empty into the slave. Rock drank as a child might from a fountain, taking care to clean his master's cock with his tongue when he had finished.

After that, Dorian regularly used him for his piss. He didn't think of it as a thing which demeaned the slave, but as a sharing of something between them. Rock drank from him because he loved him.

One day, he thought, I will drink from *him*.

There – he had said it, if only to himself. For, much as Dorian loved loving Rock, he knew, underneath, he would rather they were in the reverse positions. Dorian ached to acknowledge Rock's masculinity by capitulating to it. He wanted to crawl on the ground before that graceful, muscular body and lick Rock's feet. He wanted to feel Rock's penis, hard, inside his own bowels. He wanted to taste Rock's piss gushing into his mouth.

And yet he was scared of suggesting it. He didn't know why. He didn't feel Rock would have taken any advantage of such an arrangement – any more than he had when they had admitted their love for each other. Rock would have been a master to him in the same spirit as he served him as a slave. He would have dominated the younger boy in a loving way and allowed him to worship at his feet as Dorian wanted to, without ever seeing it as a debasing thing. It would have remained a secret between them. Rock would never have tried to use it against him, but Dorian was the freeman and Rock the slave.

Must it stay this way? he thought.

He didn't know the answer.

Carlos was returning. Maybe his time with Anton would have changed him, but in the days preceding his arrival, Dorian worried how he would treat Rock. He knew Rock accepted Carlos as his part-owner and that he realised he must endure whatever was in store for him because of it. Despite their own closeness, Rock was still a piece of property and Dorian knew he was not to forget this.

He knew, too, that Rock would not be allowed to sleep at his feet every night but would have to spend time caged like an animal. He would be fucked brutally; he would be used as a convenient hole for Carlos's spunk.

Rock understood and accepted this, but Dorian would have done anything to free him from it.

Dorian dreamt one night of the time when Carlos last flogged Rock.

He saw the stripes across his broad back and remembered him hanging in chains, exhausted. Soon he would have to go through that pain regularly.

Dorian awoke from this dream with a raging hard-on. Then, with some unease, he realised that in his dream, he had been chained there with Rock and had suffered the same – worse.

He remembered the waking image of his brother's body and

felt excitement at the prospect of seeing it once again. Now Carlos had a slave, he might feel it no longer necessary to use Dorian. Dorian hoped this would not be the case, and he hated himself for the thought.

Rock

I had grown used to kind treatment. My new young master treated me as an equal and hardly ever commanded me. When he did, I was more than happy to oblige. Instead of his merely using my body, we made love together. For the first time in my life I felt proud of myself as a man and knew what it was like to please another while being pleasured myself.

I had come to learn that in all my relationships with men, one partner would dominate the other. I had been taught to regard myself always as the subordinate one. I had been sold into slavery while little more than a child and such an ingrained vision of my place in the world was going to be hugely difficult to discard.

My master, my lover, my new friend, was slowly helping me to see the other part of myself. It wasn't that he didn't see me as a slave – he did. He chained my ankle during the night, he used my mouth for his piss and my arse for his young boy's spunk. Even so, I remembered what emotions he held underneath. It was almost as though the roles the gods had allotted to us were little more than a game we played together, both of us aware of the affection between us.

More and more I detected our real status as a complete

reversal of our positions. More than equal love, he wanted me to be in control of him. He would rather he had been the slave and I the master.

It was nothing specific. Perhaps the way he felt his way over my bare chest – almost coquettish, glancing into my eyes with the look of one who tantalises in the expectation of some brutal return. Sometimes he would lie back as I massaged his body; he would spread his arms above his head and allow me to suck on his firm young meat. I could tell, without his saying it, he was fantasising. In his dreams, his body was restrained by ropes and I was forcing him to accept my mouth round his dick. Then he would suddenly change and look ashamed.

For a while he would be quiet, then he would debase me in some small way – strike my arse with his belt, or take my balls tightly in his hand and squeeze them. These assertions of his authority (for such is what I took them to be) were neither painful nor prolonged, but they betrayed him all the same.

I had been warned about the brother's return. I had been told, in law, I belonged equally to the two of them and, where my younger master was kind, my older one was cruel.

Soon, he would arrive back from the island where their father had bought me. I dreaded the day. I remembered too well how much the older boy had enjoyed punishing me the last time. I had little doubt I was to receive many such beatings and worse.

The day arrived.

The boy, still at an age when most are only just forming their character, was brutal in the extreme. He walked swiftly into the room where I had been set to work cleaning and cooking. Without my having done anything to deserve it, he dealt me a hefty blow across the face, knocking me to the floor. I am taller than he is and stronger. Had it not been for the impossibility of getting away with it, I would have responded. This treatment was not right or fair.

I had suffered a whipping at his hands and had taken it because, then, I had deserved to be whipped. I had done wrong or, at least, I had broken the rules which had been clearly laid down. Even so, to be punished by one who took such a clear delight in his task made me uneasy. Yes, I am a slave and as such am about as low down the scale of things as I could be, but I still retain my secret pride in myself as a man.

He crouched by me and removed a sharp knife from his belt. For one moment I thought this was going to be a fight for my life. I was going to *have* to overpower him and, hopeless though it was, make my bid for freedom.

He must have known what was going through my mind. His bravery was only skin-deep for he didn't leave me with this impression for long. Clearly, he realised to do so would be playing with fire – with his own life.

Instead, he grabbed a handful of my hair and cut it off, close to my scalp.

'I'm not having my slaves looking so effeminate,' he said. 'You should look like what you are: a prisoner. Low-down scum.'

Before he proceeded, he took a couple of lengths of rope from round his waist. Still not sure whether or not I was going to retaliate, he pulled my arms behind me and bound them tightly. The other piece of rope was tied around my chest, pinioning my upper arms to my sides.

Then he proceeded to cut off my hair. I wouldn't have reacted to this, even if I had been allowed the possibility of doing so. It wasn't for me to say if I should be allowed hair on my head or my body.

The worst was yet to come.

I was taken to a yard. It was evidently a place of torture. The youth made me stand, legs apart, in the middle of a frame to which he fixed my ankles. That done, he tied my genitals tightly with some twine. My balls were thus caused to bounce against my inner thigh, tight and full. I was to be made aware of them and the possibilities they held both for my pain and my tormentor's pleasure. He had left my pubes on me, but had taken some delight in pulling a few of them out of my groin with his fingers.

I tried not to let him see the tears welling up in my eyes. They were not tears of cowardice; they were the natural response to the pain.

He fixed the end of the twine to something in the ground. My sensitised testicles were pulled downward by it. I tried to ease this by bending my legs, but he slapped my face and told me to stand straight.

Then he put a blindfold across my eyes and a gag in my mouth. I was unable to see him take two large clips from somewhere, but I soon felt their excruciating bite – one on each of my nipples. The sensation spread across my chest, culminating in two sharp points of pleasure and pain in my tortured nipples.

The clips were not enough for him. Just as I thought the hurt had gone beyond what I could take, he increased it by chaining them together.

I had been yelling through the gag, pulling away from him in my bonds. He had held me around the small of my back to prevent my falling over. Now, when all I had left in me was a pathetic whimper, he released his hold. I stood, held securely in my bonds, the pain indistinguishable from the sexual arousal which I could not deny but wanted so much to resist.

'It's not over yet,' he said. His voice sounded calm and reasonable, as though he were describing something which affected neither of us.

After pausing to take in my degradation, he added, 'Do you remember the last time I used a lash on you?'

I couldn't speak of course, but evidently some response was necessary to satisfy him. He launched his fist into my stomach and I fell backward, wrenching my ankles, which held in their manacles. My balls were yanked by the twine. Painful though this was, I was physically aware of my erection. It was as though my lower body was telling him not to believe the expression of pain and contempt which he must have been able to read in my face.

'Do you, slave?' he yelled.

I tried to struggle to my feet, but I couldn't. He pulled me up, his fingernails digging into the flesh of my upper arms.

The hurt in my stomach was a counter to the sharper, needling pain in my nipples. As this subsided, it was supplanted by a fiery feeling of lust which burnt across me, following the path made by the chain which linked my pectoral muscles.

I nodded, trying to breathe deeply in order to take what he dealt me without breaking. I determined that, somehow, I wasn't going to let this young thug have the pleasure of seeing me weep.

'Well, this is a reminder of it,' he said.

He began to lash my buttocks with his whip. I tried desperately to stand my ground. I even attempted to stand straight, not to give in to the desire to ease the pull on my testicles. I tried to think about other things: anything other than when the next crack of his whip would land on me. Through-out, my penis betrayed me, hard and demanding. It seemed to be asking him for more pain, more humiliation.

He didn't concentrate wholly on my backside. He used the more tender, sensitive flesh, lower down on my thighs, almost as viciously. I thought I would die from the agony of it.

Somehow I managed not to come.

It stopped at last. I was not released and taken away to recover as my previous master would have allowed. He simply stopped, as suddenly as he had begun.

I swore to myself I would have revenge for this.

My flesh continued to cry out. My brain was confused as to which part of me hurt the most, and whether it was the burning across my chest or my backside which fed my lust for more.

Soon I had gone beyond this feeling. I felt as though I were floating away from myself. There, far below, I could imagine my body, vulnerable and bound. I pictured my own tears rolling down from behind the blindfold, but they didn't seem to belong to me.

From where I was in my imagination, far away, I could see my torturer take a long, slim implement made of smooth and polished wood. It was thin at one end but increased in girth gradually along its length.

I knew what was about to happen.

Sure enough, he pushed the implement (or maybe it was some similar phallus) into my rectum, delighting in the unfeeling, instinctive response my poor body made to this invasion. I heard my own muffled screams.

When the thing was completely inside my gut, the boy stripped himself and stood in front of his handiwork. With my ghost-eyes, I saw him masturbate in front of his prisoner's wrecked physique. As he reached his climax he moved close to my body. Semen hit my abdomen: so far, the only area of flesh he had not violated.

Then he picked up his clothing and left me alone.

Eight

Dorian had been at his studies all day and had arrived home in the early evening looking forward, as usual, to his time with Rock by the pool. He had left his slave-lover working on some domestic chores. He'd ceased to bother fettering him during the day: he knew Rock would make no attempt to escape. Even at night, the ankle chain seemed extraneous, but Dorian liked to see it there and had not yet given it up. Rock was always obedient and never made any comment, whether he was chained or not.

Dorian was surprised, therefore, not to find him where he expected him to be. He called Rock's name and received no answer.

He gave way to a sudden feeling of panic. Had his beautiful boy escaped? Escaped from what? From him, Dorian? From slavery? And to what?

No, he told himself, it was impossible. Rock would never do such a thing. The slave's feelings of loyalty to his young master were as strong as any chains. Besides, he knew he would never get very far. He could expect either to be recaptured and returned, or to be stolen by a trader and sold to somebody else. Most likely he would find himself in the hands of a slaver who cared nothing for him beyond the obvious financial value he had.

His absence, then, could only mean one thing: Carlos was home.

Dorian went over to his brother's part of the house. His heart was thumping. He didn't really have to stretch his imagination to guess what he would find, and it wasn't as though Rock hadn't been warned and prepared. All the same, he didn't want Rock to have to suffer.

Dorian considered volunteering his own body in Rock's place, but he was more than likely going to be too late.

He arrived at Carlos's door and knocked. There was no reply. He tried the handle. It turned: the door was not locked. It was true then. Carlos was home.

Inside, the curtains were drawn against the strong, early-evening sun. The bed was made up with white, light cotton sheets and a heavier, red counterpane. There was no sign of anyone.

'Carlos!' he called, still hoping to get no reply. 'Carlos, are you back?'

Dorian ventured further into the room; it was indeed empty. He crossed over and pushed open the small door at the back and went down the three or four stairs into the dressing room. It, too, was empty, although clothes were scattered about on the floor. He looked towards the wall where Carlos proudly displayed his special whip and his belts. He always maintained he kept them there as a warning to his subordinates – and to his brother. Dorian had always known this to be only partly true. Carlos liked to see them because they gave him a feeling of power.

They were gone.

Their absence confirmed what Dorian had supposed: Carlos was using them. Dorian knew who the unfortunate recipient would surely be.

At the back of the house was a small yard which Carlos had long ago claimed as his own space. Dorian had never known if their father was aware of why he'd wanted it.

As soon as the yard had become his, Carlos had begun to create a place which must have existed in his fantasies all along.

The space was surrounded by a high wall and flagged with concrete slabs. Carlos fixed metal brackets into the masonry at just above the average height of a man. He installed an iron cage, a small, cramped thing where his victims would have to squat with their heads forced down by the bars above them. It had probably been used for large dogs or similar-sized animals. It wasn't big enough to contain a human, but this was evidently what it was now intended for.

Carlos had erected a framework in the centre of the yard. It was similar to a door-frame, but it had double sets of manacles at each of its four corners. An iron ring was driven into the concrete in the centre of the ground beneath this contraption.

He had bought chains and ropes, belts, whips, canes, branding-irons, vicious clips and leashes. All these implements were on view, displayed on the wall – a more fearful reflection of his bedroom array.

Dorian knew this was where he should next look for Rock.

The yard was bathed in evening light. The flagstones which covered the ground were uncomfortably hot, but Rock had not been allowed to wear anything on his feet.

His hands were pulled behind his back in the most awkward way possible. They were bound together with thick rope. His upper arms and chest were similarly tied. His legs were spread and fastened to the manacles at each foot of the framework. In between these, a piece of black twine was tied at one end to the central iron ring. At the other it was wrapped around the base of his cock, encircling his balls and dividing them into two swollen, purple orbs.

His nipples had been put into metal clamps and these were attached one to the other with a thin chain which was just heavy enough to pull on each, making the sensation constant.

Dorian had allowed Rock to grow his hair back. It had become thick and long, bleached fair by the sun, framing his face as it fell in waves around his head. Now, it had been shaved again, closely cropped, a sign of penitence for a crime he had never committed.

He was blindfold and gagged. His body, even parts of the front of him, was covered in red weals and angry stripes. As Dorian approached, he tried to shift his balance. The way his legs were restrained would not allow him to do so. He staggered slightly. Dorian went round behind him and gasped as he saw the patterns of the lash on his buttocks. He must have suffered thirty or forty strokes at least. Dorian's emotions swerved between feeling for his friend's pain and a rising erotic response which he was very aware was taking over his own genitals.

Rock's arse was plugged. Dorian reached and pulled on the phallus. He still hadn't spoken and, Rock, assuming he was about to receive more pain, tensed his body. His chest filled out as he hissed air in through his gag, at the same time, jerking his blinded face upward.

'It's me, Dorian,' said the other. 'Let me take it out.'

He pulled as gently as he could and Rock's guts expelled a truncheon nearly as big as a man's forearm. He whimpered as it came out. His hole was big, raw and gaping.

Dorian undid his feet and Rock collapsed on to his knees. He was still beautiful. Gagged and bound, bruised, blindfold and shorn, he yet retained his masculine power.

Dorian was about to free his friend properly and take him back to attend to the wounds when a voice stopped him.

'Well, well, well. My little brother's come to steal back my slave. What are we to do now?'

Dorian turned to look into the face of his brother, Carlos.

'He belongs to both of us,' Dorian began, trying to make his voice sound casual – as though he had been discovered with some jointly owned toy when it was not strictly his turn to have it. He was hoping to treat the situation lightly and get a similar response back. He must have known there was little or no hope of this. Carlos delighted in humiliating others. One of his favourite pastimes was humiliating those he considered inferior. Dorian was not going to be spared.

Even though, within their father's eyes and within the law, the brothers were equal, Dorian still feared Carlos. He hoped their time apart would mark a division in their relationship. Before, his brother had been able to use him; now Dorian had reached early adulthood and he wanted to be seen as a man. Despite this, despite Dorian's adult body and his recent discovery that he had grown as tall as his brother, he felt little more than Carlos's chattel.

Again there was that brief but increasingly nagging doubt: did he resent this? Or was it what he wanted?

Carlos was tanned from his time away and he looked somehow more mature. He wore a baggy white shirt, open down to his navel. It was tucked into tight breeches which outlined what looked like a hard-on. (Having had Carlos's whole meat inside him, Dorian knew that cock was big enough to look hard even when completely flaccid.) His brother's blue eyes were cold and amused.

In spite of what he had done to Rock, Dorian was taken by how handsome Carlos was. His jet-black hair was longer than he had been wont to grow it. It made his face seem thinner and complemented the inky beauty of his eyes. People used to say the two brothers looked alike. Dorian could acknowledge a physical resemblance but he maintained always that their personalities made a difference to the way they looked. He and Carlos were darkness and light, hard and soft, maybe even good and bad. The sadism which characterised the older boy was a visible, sexual thing. It was there in his looks and in his demeanour. It was a powerful thing and one which excited Dorian beyond reason; he could never deny it.

Carlos approached and placed his hand on the back of his brother's neck. The gesture seemed tender but the other was suspicious of it and afraid. Carlos brought Dorian's face close to his own and kissed him full on the lips. Dorian was still too wary to respond. Carlos pulled away and looked the younger boy straight in the eye.

'Not willing to greet me on my first day back home? That's not very kind of you.'

Dorian knelt down in front of him and kissed his feet. He thought this humbling of himself might be appreciated. He thought Carlos might relent and allow him to take Rock away.

'Please, Carlos, sir. Please may I take the slave back with me now? I need him for – something . . .'

'Something? What something?' Carlos took Rock's chin in his hand and pulled the slave's blinded eyes upward towards his own face. 'My little brother wants you for something. To punish you again, I shouldn't wonder.' He addressed Dorian. 'Is that what you want him for?'

'No. He, he has some domestic duties to perform.'

'And how do I know you're not going to pamper him and take away all the good I have just done?'

He turned again to Rock, who whimpered as Carlos's hand caressed his cheek. Carlos continued to talk to Dorian, but kept his eyes on his prisoner, taking in the results of his earlier pleasure.

'It's a form of cruelty really, you know. His skin had become so soft it was hardly able to take the whipping. Look at the bruises on his arse-cheeks. A slave's backside should be like leather. I should be able to give him twice as much before he breaks.'

'We agreed I should have him as much as you. Can it not be my turn now?'

Carlos suddenly dropped the pretence of being reasonable.

'You've had him for the past few weeks. He's mine for as long as I want him. You've spoiled him enough. Anyway, I have something in mind for the three of us to enjoy.'

Dorian was still at his feet. Carlos lowered his body to the supplicant's eye level and took his brother's face in both his hands. Dorian knew Carlos found him attractive and enjoyed

looking at him, but still felt uncomfortable when he demonstrated it.

He lowered his eyes respectfully and allowed his brother to
brush a hand lightly over his face. Then, still gently, Carlos
unbuttoned Dorian's shirt and lowered it off his shoulders. He
ran his hands over the front of the exposed chest, stopping at
the nipples and squeezing gently. Then, all of a sudden, he
appeared to tire of this. He rose to his feet.

'Lower your breeches, quickly.'

Dorian did as he was told. He stood there in his underwear,
head still bowed and his body trembling; he didn't know
whether this was from fear or anticipation.

Carlos went over to a large box in the corner of the yard.
While his back was turned, Dorian was able, briefly, to run a
hand over Rock's head. A gesture of friendship and support:
futile but the best that could be offered.

Carlos approached from behind. His hands reached round
and gave Dorian's nipples another light squeeze. This continued
gentleness was surprising: he usually wanted to get straight on
to hurting his victims. The control he exercised was reminiscent
of a cat playing with a mouse.

His arms still holding on to his brother's nipples, he pulled
the younger boy backward against his own chest. He pressed
his head against Dorian's neck and kissed him along the jawline.

'Oh, little brother,' he whispered, 'I've missed you.'

This was a shock. In all those years Dorian had never
appreciated till then that Carlos's rough treatment was, to him,
a form of lovemaking. Dorian knew Carlos desired him, but
missed him? He didn't know what to do, but that was of little
matter because Carlos had decided for him.

'I'm sorry, I have to do this. You know I have to do it,' he
whispered.

Dorian prepared himself for what was to come.

He wondered all the time what Rock was thinking of this.

Rock

The elder looked so much like the younger that it would have been difficult to appreciate they were not related by blood were it not for the hard expression on the elder one's face. His eyes were of the same brown-black but, where my lover's were kind and understanding, like rare and precious stones, his were of a different season – cold and full of hate.

Their dark hair was of similar length and their bodies muscled and toned in the same manner. I couldn't imagine my lover getting into a foul mood, nor yet could I see his brother given over to sudden fits of humanity. Had either of these things ever happened, there wouldn't have been much for a man to choose between them.

My blindfold had been removed. My out-of-body experience seemed like a dream: perhaps it had been. Now all I felt was a dull, constant aching. Sexual release was still uppermost in part of my mind. My cock was still absolutely erect. Other parts of my body and my brain screamed their protest. I was wretched, but now I had my lover here there was a chance of release for both my semen and my tortured limbs. It was clear to me the older boy had the upper hand and it also seemed the younger was more than a little afraid of him. Yet I had to hope.

It was not to be.

After what seemed like an affectionate greeting, the elder boy commanded Dorian to strip down to his underwear. This instruction was obeyed uncomplainingly, with a kind of resigned dismay on that handsome face.

Dorian's body was truly wonderful, everything from his sculptured shoulders to his sturdy, hairy, legs.

His organ and balls were wrapped loosely in his customary loincloth above which his stomach rippled as he breathed quickly and nervously. This also made his pectorals – powerful and decorated with large, smooth, pink nipples – rise and fall gently. A light dusting of hair covered his upper chest. He shaved his face but was not without a slight growth of stubble over the front of his long, thick neck and square jaw.

He reminded me of a stag which has been cornered by hunters and knows it must suffer, but retains the proud dignity of its physical magnificence in the face of danger.

Carlos (for that was the name of the elder one) had my lover go and get restraints from a box in the corner of the yard. Again, this command was obeyed. He made the boy kneel and present the ropes which would soon bind his hands. After this, he manhandled him towards the structure of posts from which Dorian had only just released me. He was fixed to it, crucified, arms and legs spread to the four corners.

'Now you'll be able to watch and see how much your little master can take,' Carlos said to me.

This struck me as obscene. Not only was Dorian a freeman, but the two of them were of the same family. I was surprised, too, that the preparations for this horrid scene had been carried out so meekly. It appeared this was not the first time my lover had had to suffer this indignity. If I'd taken even as much as half the punishment I had, I would have willingly gone in Dorian's place. As it was, I was spent and all I could do was whimper hopelessly.

'Your slave has taken some of your punishment,' Carlos

went on, addressing his brother. 'I told him I would use you to finish off whatever he couldn't take.'

This was a lie; he had said no such thing. The sadist was playing with Dorian's mind. He continued with his own version of what had happened to me.

'He fainted, but not before he'd had the brunt of it. However, I think we can still mark you a bit.'

I lowered my head, not wanting to watch, but Carlos lifted it up and slapped me soundly across both cheeks.

'Watch,' he said.

He took a whip from a hook on the wall. He placed it before his brother's mouth and made him kiss it. Then he cracked it several times before striking it across his brother's broad back.

My lover cried out. I already wanted to hold him, to comfort him. A red mark crossed his lovely shoulders. In a second another appeared, crossing the first. Then another and another. Carlos did not vary the weight of the blows: each was cruel and hard. My young master yelled but did not plead for him to stop. I realised he was weeping. Each time, I could see his body preparing for the next blow, trying to be ready, trying to be strong against it. Then it would come and his powerful young frame would collapse within his bonds, pain taking over the will to appear impervious.

When his back was as well covered with welts as I supposed my own arse to be, Carlos went over and impatiently snatched away the underwear from his brother's waist.

Those naked buttocks, hard and round. They almost invited contact. But where I wanted to kiss them and bury my face between them, Carlos only wanted to hurt them.

He used a belt for this. The whip had been used across my own arse and I was glad that Dorian was to be spared this. Still, Carlos did not ease his punishment. He frequently laughed, citing his victim's undeniably erect penis as proof of his being no more than a slave at heart.

Then he was finished. He dragged me over and pushed my face into Dorian's groin. I tried to get the hard cock into my mouth, to at least give my master some pleasure, but I was pulled away almost as quickly as I had been pushed towards it.

My hands were still tied behind me. Carlos undid them and made me stand. I was then fixed to match his other prisoner. Each of my wrists and ankles was fixed next to his: the double manacles on each corner of the frame held our bodies together, facing each other. I wanted to kiss my master, but I knew I must wait until we were alone.

Carlos then took some rawhide and tied it round our testicles. He passed the thin binding round the base of each of our cocks and pulled it tight. That beautiful union of our sex was now another point of discomfort and humiliation. Obscene – forced upon us, where before it had been an expression of our love.

Next, he attended to our nipples. He used the same sort of clips on his brother's as he did on me, crossing two chains between us, linking our pectorals with an X shape of metal links.

He finished by fixing thin, metal collars around our necks and linking these to each other with another chain. Both of us were totally unable to move without hurting ourselves and the other in the attempt.

'I'll leave you there for a while,' he said. 'Happy dreams.'

Nine

The sea was calm. Justin was glad of it for he was no sailor. Since his new life had begun, he had prided himself on being able to quickly learn all the skills his new companions had grown up with. He had become an expert with the sword; he was the outright winner of most sporting matches; he had learnt to read and had become something of a scholar. He had even taught himself to recognise the birds, animals and flora of the woods around the mountains which were now his home.

Despite all this, he hadn't been blessed with 'sea legs'. He watched the shore growing closer and closer. It was the first time since that fateful market day he'd been anywhere near to these islands. He had no wish to return. In fact, the ship's company had no plans to set foot on Illyrian soil. Their destination was some way from the land of Justin's slavery. He hoped his companions were correct and this self-imposed mission of duty would have a successful result.

Those years he'd spent as the property of another man seemed like a lifetime ago. He often remembered the time when his nakedness had been paraded in front of the lustful eyes of men who could take him whenever they chose. Justin's golden body was now his own and he took the clothing he wore for granted. At first it had seemed strange to be covered and it had taken him some time to stop thinking of himself as a sexual object, there for the taking. Now, he had become used to his new self. He even bathed in private.

And he was happy to have his adored Xania by his side.

At their first meeting, she had both terrified and excited him. Tall women had always been his secret desire. Xania's height was accentuated by her thin frame and fine bones. Her copper-coloured hair fell about her face and down her back, giving her the look of a beautiful enchantress. He had thought her the most enticing creature he had ever seen.

On that first day, as she stepped off the boat on to the Illyrian shore, he had instinctively prostrated himself on the sand, realising straight away this was the person who had bought him.

His companion on the road from the market had hinted that he was no longer to be a slave. If this turned out to be a lie, at least he would now be a willing plaything. The man was right: no chains were necessary to keep him in the service of this fascinating woman.

'Have you not been told? You can dispense with all that nonsense. You're a free man. Get up.'

Her voice was deep and musical. It had a natural air of command and yet it was also friendly. Justin raised his eyes. She was looking at him carefully, judging his reaction to her words. He slowly rose and stood facing her. She was as tall as he was. Her skin was brown, tanned by the wind and the sun. Her robe, wet with seawater around the hem, was of a heavy, expensive but rough material. She wore no jewellery.

'I am Xania. You are welcome.'

He kissed her hand. She smiled at this courtly gesture, then turned to Justin's companion.

'You've done well, Godfrey. Now let's get back to where we belong. I'm bored with this shoreline. Justin – that is your name is it not?'

Justin nodded. 'Yes, ma'am,' he said.

She seemed to approve of the salutation. 'Good,' she went

on. 'Justin – I hope and trust you are willing to accompany us. You don't have to. You are not going to be forced, but after the company of all these brutes –' Godfrey laughed with her at this description '– after nothing but hairy warriors to look at, your fair curls will be a welcome change.'

Justin hoped this was intended to be as suggestive as it sounded. He agreed readily. The three of them waded through the lapping, shallow water towards the boat.

So Justin's new life began.

Once they had put out to sea, Justin was sent for. Over the few hours the journey took, he was told of his new home and the people who were taking him to it.

'My grandfather was a great lord,' Xania said. 'He owned lands not far from here and my father grew up with expectations of becoming his heir.'

She suddenly looked sad, lost in thought, but she brought herself back to the present with a sudden, obvious determination.

'My grandfather was taken by the Illyrians. It was only because of a servant's loyalty that Father managed to escape. He was smuggled out of the castle by way of a secret route and taken into the mountains where he would be safe. He never heard of my grandfather again. I suspect that, like you, he was taken into slavery. In any case, he must have perished long ago.

'My father created a settlement, there in the mountains. Not long after he was joined by others who were fleeing from the tyranny of the Illyrian people. This was a generation ago, when the Illyrians were still set on conquering all around them. I suppose we've all learnt to live alongside each other since.'

She smiled and patted Justin's knee. 'Do not take offence, but I use the slave market as I used to use the animal shop when I was a small girl. I spent everything I had on animals, which I set free as soon as we were out of the door.'

'I am an animal then?' Justin said, taking care not to sound offended by the idea. Indeed, he wasn't. If it meant an end to his bondage he would be whatever this lady wanted.

'Are you?' she asked salaciously. She smiled and put her hand over his.

'Why me?' Justin asked. 'I was only one of many slaves.'

She shrugged. 'I was among the crowds at the market and I took time to judge where best my little money could be spent. There are plenty who derive pleasure from being taken by another man and some who even relish the whip. You did not. I could see that.'

'They may derive pleasure from men, but surely it should be of their own choice who it is that invades their arses.' Justin stopped, aware of the unprovoked anger in his voice.

'I'm sorry,' he went on. 'I have friends who are still there. Their cocks might always be in agreement with their minds.'

She smiled. 'I can see your anger and understand it. We too have men who enjoy the bodies of their own sex. I have no quarrel with that. We too use the lash to punish malefactors. I have no quarrel with that. But, like you, I think a human should choose his sexual partners and I don't think unwilling and innocent men should be whipped merely for the entertainment of others. I don't deny the pleasure to be got from the Illyrians' way of life, but I think such pleasure has to be extended to all parties.'

She stopped, and looked at him again, still smiling. 'These friends of yours. Perhaps we could help them.'

'I don't know where they've been taken. They could be anywhere.'

'They were sold at the same time as you?'

He nodded. For some reason his old companions suddenly seemed very important to him. He had not realised how much he cared about them until then. He remembered all the small kindnesses Rock and Theo had performed to ease his pains. They often took more than their fair share of punishment to save him. Many times they had presented themselves to be fucked in his place. He had always assumed this to be right and

126

proper. They enjoyed it and he did not. Now he realised there must have been many occasions when their actions were not dictated by their own pleasure, but out of concern for him.

'We'll make enquiries,' Xania said. 'I have ways of finding out where slaves end up.' She laughed. 'Don't look so impressed. Did you not know? They keep a register. All one has to do is look in it.'

Her amusement made her even more attractive. Justin had not had sexual contact with a woman for many years and his cock was responding to the sight of her.

'To choose my own sexual partners,' he said. 'You're right. It's the thing I've wanted all these years.'

She slipped her robe from off her shoulders. Underneath she was naked.

'It's your choice,' she said. 'I offer it to you.'

And now, some months later, he was Xania's official partner. She had been as good as her word and had sent a man into Illyria to find out who had bought his two friends. Justin recognised Rock's owner's name straight away. All that time ago in Anton's yard: Rock secured to the whipping-post, his skin a mass of red welts and bruises, and a young boy with the whip still in his hand. It was the same surname.

Not knowing what they would find, they were now sailing towards a seemingly unprotected villa where, if the register was correct, Rock would be one of the house-slaves. Justin was for an all-out assault on the place but Xania had pointed out they didn't yet know any injustice had occurred. They must find out whether they had any good reason to attack.

'We're not despots,' she said. 'See, the house looks peaceful enough. Perhaps your friend has found happiness here after all.'

Justin had to agree. Perhaps he was being hasty. He remembered another boy: a brother. He had kissed Rock and looked on him kindly. During his own captivity, many of the slaves he had met had been more than content with their lives. A great number would not have exchanged their positions for freedom even if it had been offered.

For all his hopes that everything would be well, he had his sword ready. He had picked the best fighters to go with them. They were prepared for every eventuality.

Rock and Dorian knew nothing. Miserable, racked with the pains of their torment, they pressed their bodies close together and tried to comfort each other as best they could. They feared Carlos's return. Would he have had enough? Or would he want to break them even further?

An hour had passed. Dorian tried to reassure Rock. He told him Carlos rarely took his fantasies to such extremes. He would surely have sated his lustful appetite by now. He wasn't sure if Rock took in his words: he was still gagged, and his eyes had glazed over. Dorian hoped he had fainted; at least his wounds would not hurt him then.

Dorian, too, must have drifted into some sort of half-faint, half-sleep. He woke some time later and was surprised to hear the sounds of other people in the building. Shouts could be heard; they seemed a long way off. The evening air was still and the voices carried clearly enough, although the words were unfamiliar, foreign perhaps. At first he thought he must be hallucinating.

The noises grew nearer. Dorian heard running steps and the banging of doors. Whoever it was must surely be in the building without permission.

His heart began to race. Maybe the house was under attack! He hoped and prayed Carlos would come and release them, give them some chance of escape. Surley he wouldn't leave them there, bound and naked, unarmed? Carlos might not care a jot for Rock, but Dorian was his brother. Was he going to leave his own brother to die at the hands of these unseen enemies?

Time passed. It seemed like forever but was in fact only a

few minutes. Rock was awake once more. His eyes were now alert to the danger – he tried to speak.

'I don't know,' Dorian said desperately. 'I don't know what's happening. Try not to move. We can't do anything.'

This was said as much for himself as for Rock. Each time Rock pulled away from him, the movement caused a strain on the nipple-clamps, sending agonising stabs shooting through the tender parts of both their bodies.

'We can't do anything,' Dorian repeated. 'We must hope somebody – my brother even – frees us and we have a chance to escape.'

However, it was not Carlos who came.

The place where they were held was not easily found, and unknown to the prisoners they were very nearly overlooked. Had not one of Xania's men accidentally found the door to the yard, they would have been left. Carlos would, no doubt, have had the apologies of the intruders and all three lives would have taken a different course.

The visitor to the yard was grizzled and swarthy. His sword was ready in his hand and his body was covered in dirt and sweat. The armour he wore was crude. It was made from thick leather, strapped around his body over some sort of rough grey tunic. A more unlikely looking saviour was hard to imagine. He looked as ready to decapitate the two victims as show the slightest hint of concern.

He didn't speak. For what seemed like and eternity, he stood where he had entered, sword drawn, eyes darting this way and that as though he expected hidden opponents to fall from the skies or leap out of the walls.

He circled them, keeping his distance. Dorian guessed he feared they were the bait in some sort of trap. Having satisfied himself of his safety, he approached and, with an expression of curiosity on his rugged face, he gently laid a hand on Rock's back.

Even a light touch was enough to awaken the potential of

129

each wound: Rock lurched. Dorian tried not to show his agony as his nipples were yanked and his balls pulled with Rock's. The man quickly withdrew.

Having assessed their predicament, he took a knife from his belt and set about freeing them from their bonds. Neither was able to stand. They simply collapsed on the ground and lay there, helpless, expecting at any moment for the knife to finish its work by putting them out of their misery.

The blow never came. The soldier hollered something which brought two others to his side.

His language was not one Dorian knew. He supposed him to be from one of the lands to the north of their country.

When he switched to familiar language, his accent sounded slightly ludicrous, like someone doing an imitation of a foreigner.

'We'll get something to carry you on,' he said. Under the strange accent, his tone was sure and not to be questioned. He knelt beside them. 'Can you understand what I say?'

Dorian nodded. Rock stayed absolutely still. He was used to others being the ones permitted to respond to such questions.

'It looks as though you've had a terrible wrong done to you. It's over now. I am your liberator.'

The two men returned, carrying between them a roughly improvised stretcher. Close behind came another, ready to carry them away.

The last man was familiar to Dorian; he was not in any way physically like his comrades. Where they were dark, he was blond; where they were rough and animal-like, he was toned and smooth. He had the body of an athlete, not a warrior. Even so, he was dressed in the same way as the others and was clearly one of them.

As soon as he entered the yard, Rock's eyes filled with tears and his hand tightened on Dorian's. His face was suddenly transformed with the pleasure of recognition. As the stranger stopped short of them, surprise and bewilderment radiated from him.

Rock's voice was cracked and tearful.

'Is it really you?' he gasped. 'I thought I'd never see you again.'

The stranger rushed to him and grasped his other hand.

'You're safe now,' he said. 'You're safe.'

He turned to the others. 'We must find the person who's done this to them. Search the rooms. We have our evidence now.'

Earlier, Carlos had been quite unaware of the boat approaching the shores near his father's house. In his mind, he had the image of his brother and that beautiful slave, both of them entirely at his mercy, both smarting from the whipping he had just dealt them. He intended to return later and plunge his cock into one, or both, of those inviting arses.

It was tempting to lie down and have a wank. He was sure it wouldn't take long for him to come, but he wanted to hold it back. The mild, pleasant torment of anticipation would make the act of fucking his prisoners all the more enjoyable when he eventually indulged himself. Meanwhile, his two victims could stay where they were and he would relish the thought of their hanging there.

For some reason, the picture of his brother's nipples kept recurring in his imagination. Those clips and the chains – so wonderful against the soft, tender points on that smooth young chest. His hand brushed over his groin and he gave his erection a comforting squeeze. Could he wait? Yes, he deserved to savour this – he would wait.

He stripped to his underwear and lay face downward on his bed. He allowed his cock to rub against the mattress. It was a comforting feeling. The material of his underwear caressed his genitals. His balls were tickled gently by the hairs that covered them. His penis glowed with the pleasure of it. He let out a deep contented sigh and drifted slowly into sleep.

An hour must have passed. The sun was lower in the sky. Carlos awoke to the sounds of footsteps running down the stone corridors outside his room. He should have been alone in the house, save for his two prisoners. A door was banged shut and an unfamiliar man's voice called something in a foreign language.

Carlos was alert at once. He rose and padded over the cold floor of his room, and opened the door slowly and quietly. Something was wrong, he was sure of it. None of the servants should have been around that day and his father's slaves were with the old man, far away, visiting some friend of the family. He reached for a weapon. The only thing which came to hand was a stick which he had intended to fashion into a plug for a man's arse – probably the new slave's, but perhaps his brother's. He grasped it tightly. It wasn't much by way of protection, but it was something.

Still dressed only in his underwear, he crept along the corridor. He didn't get far. The door at the end of the passage was flung open and Carlos was greeted by two men. They were both taller and broader than he and both were dark-skinned, rough and hairy. Their chests, legs and arms were magnificent and, were it not for their chiseled faces, he would have thought them beautiful. However, he was not going to be allowed to appreciate their physical attributes. One nodded to the other before they grabbed him by each arm. He didn't have time to protest or defend himself. Within seconds he was overpowered, his hands were secured behind his back and he was pushed along the corridors to the main outer door.

Rock

Justin was the last person on God's earth I had expected to see. I had never been close to him in the way I was to Theo, but I had thought of him more than once and hoped he had found a caring master.

His former, sometimes truculent manner had gone. He seemed almost tearful at our reunion. He released both of us from our bonds and sent his companion to find a couple of blankets to cover our nakedness. At the time I must have thought this modesty odd, but I don't remember commenting on it. I was just relieved to see a friendly face and to be set free. My body was almost unable to support itself and I could see Dorian was close to the same state of exhaustion.

Justin, previously never one to show his feelings, put an arm around me and helped me to stagger out of the yard. The other man did the same for Dorian. I wanted to ask how this circumstance had come about: how Justin had found us and what had happened to bring him here. He shushed me as soon as I tried to talk.

'We'll have time for that later. You must rest first. They've treated you badly but it's over now.'

He kept up his reassuring words as he led me out of the villa.

133

There were others outside, all of them brawny, warlike types, they murmured among themselves as Dorian and I were helped down the rocky path towards the beach.

There was a ship waiting. The other bandits (if that's what they were) followed us down towards it. On the beach three of them surrounded a huddled, naked figure. This man's hands were tied behind him and he had been forced at swordpoint to kneel. His face had been pushed into the sand. His captors kept very close to him and his broad back quivered with fear. I didn't need to see his face – it was Carlos.

Dorian recognised his brother at once. He was about to say something but I quickly turned and silenced him with a warning glance. Despite Justin's presence amongst them, we didn't yet know who our benefactors really were. For all I could guess, Dorian might be in as much danger as Carlos. He was, after all, one of the family they had just raided. I prayed his physical resemblance to their prisoner would not excite their curiosity. Justin called to the group guarding the prostrate captive.

'Only one? Where are the others?'

One of the men grinned and poked Carlos with his foot.

'Only one, but he's a good 'un. The house was empty apart from him. He must be the one you're looking for all right. Perhaps your friends will confirm it?'

Justin indicated to the man to show him the captive's face. Carlos was made to look up, but kept his eyes tight shut. I was strangely thankful for this. I didn't want him to see us.

Justin nodded. 'I don't need confirmation. I know him. We have the right person.'

We were helped onto the ship. Justin showed us to a clean and comfortable cabin containing two berths.

'You can sleep here,' he said. 'I'll bring you some food presently. Do you need anything else?'

'No,' I replied. 'I think sleep will help.'

Justin came close to me and, to my surprise, kissed me full on the lips.

'You were always good to me,' he said. 'Now I can repay you. Sleep for as long as you need.'

At the door he turned to the still-silent Dorian.

'I know who you are,' he said. 'But you need not fear. Whatever reason that bastard had to treat you as he did, I think we can safely welcome you as a friend. If you wish to rest with each other, pull the beds together. You won't be disturbed by anyone but me. There are some things to help your lovemaking in a box under one of the beds.'

We lay there for a long time. Following Justin's advice, we placed the two berths side by side and made a large bed from them. Dorian curled up in a foetal position with his back nestling into my chest. I put my arms around him and kissed his neck gently. Soon his breathing became regular and peaceful.

I could not sleep. My mind was racing and, to tell the truth, Dorian's body was exciting me. I let my hands wander over the tight skin of his chest. I circled his nipples with my fingers and traced the muscled path down to his navel and below. His cock was hard. I stroked it gently, holding it between two fingers of my right hand while using my left to caress his torso. He stirred slightly but didn't wake. I pushed my groin into the cleft between his buttocks and rubbed my dick up and down the inviting valley, pushing gently at the place where I sensed his hole to be. I wanted to put myself inside him but I decided to save that till later.

He was no longer my master. Sleeping in that trusting, gentle position, he was the lover I had longed for him to be. I squeezed his gorgeous body, hugging him to me. He murmured in his sleep and turned over. His cock met mine and he nuzzled up to me with his face against my breast. I held him there protectively.

I slipped into a state somewhere between wakefulness and sleeping. Dreams skitted around my mind, but I was conscious

135

of where I was and that these images were only the products of my imagination.

I was floating on water. The rhythmic movements of the boat must have prompted this sensation. I was quite safe and Dorian was with me, curled as he was into my body. His cock had, either in my daydream or in reality, found its way in between my legs where, hard and hot, it prodded my perineum. He moved with the undulation of the water, in and out, slowly, wonderfully. I gripped his member with my thighs, feeling its heat and the slight stickiness of his pre-come. My own penis was flat against his stomach, his movements keeping it hard and wanting. Our arms, his tight round my neck and mine round his waist, held us together almost as if we were two parts of one being.

I felt his breath against my skin. I remembered his ordeal and felt tears coming into my eyes. How could anyone use this beautiful boy so badly, least of all his own brother? The emotion was sweet and bitter at the same time. I wanted so much to protect him, to love him. Yet I couldn't ignore the arousal I felt when I thought of him as he'd been: next to me, his hands tied near to mine, his cock bound tightly to my own, our nipples linked by those piercing clips and their chains. The pain of being beaten had drifted into the back of my memory. Now I only recalled the exquisite humiliation I had felt as I was lashed. This, and the aching lust which had overpowered me when I pressed myself close to Dorian as he too suffered under his brother's whip.

I felt an uncontrollable urge to take Dorian then and there. I wanted to fuck him till he pleaded for me to stop. I don't know whether it was at that moment our roles changed for ever. I had always sensed that he wanted me to be the stronger of the two of us. Now, with our social positions gone, we were equal and we could explore each other's needs as we wished.

I gently pushed Dorian's head down my body towards my penis. He opened his eyes and tried to say something. I responded by filling his mouth with my organ. He sucked eagerly: licking across the top of my knob with quick, fleeting darts, sometimes pressing his tongue into my piss-slit before swallowing the whole prick, and cupping his hands under my balls as he did so. I lay there savouring the sensations, holding his head so that when he tried to stop or come up for air he was unable to do so. I pushed my cock into his throat, fucking his mouth roughly. He took it all in, opening his mouth wide to receive my eager thrusts.

When I felt my orgasm beginning to boil up inside my balls, I pulled him away and held him there, next to my groin. He looked up at me pleadingly.

'Please,' he said. 'Let me have your spunk in my mouth. Please.'

'I'm going to fuck you,' I said crudely. 'You're to have my spunk all right. But it's going up your pretty little arsehole. Turn over.'

He didn't seem to question the authority in my voice or worry that I had taken this rough tone with him. He simply obeyed my order and presented me with his firm buttocks protecting his tight little hole. I spat on my hand and eased some of the saliva in between his legs.

He pressed upward towards my finger, allowing it to enter him. I could tell that he winced as it went in, but he made no complaint. I moved my finger around inside him, probing the muscle, making him squirm.

My cock was throbbing with urgent desire. I gripped Dorian around his belly and pulled him up on to all fours. He thrust his buttocks up towards me. I pulled the cheeks apart, taking a moment or two to look upon his shit-hole.

He hadn't much hair around his arse, just enough to make the prospect of putting my dick up it a pleasurable one. I teased him slightly by probing at his entrance with the end of my tool. He responded by thrusting his arse against it, trying to impale himself on me. I dealt him a light slap across his backside, not enough to hurt him: he was still stinging from the whipping he had received. It was, however, enough to let him know that our roles had completely reversed. He could no longer command me. He must obey.

'Please,' he said. 'Please, sir. Put yourself into my arse. I beg you, sir.'

'Be patient, little boy,' I replied. Calling him that stirred something inside me. I had ceased to be a slave. He was mine now and I was in control of him and of myself. Much as I wanted to shoot my spunk inside him, I also wanted to enjoy this new me. I pushed against him again, not allowing his thrusts backward to have the effect he wanted so badly.

I pulled away from him. He continued to push his body vainly towards the place where I had been. Then he realised that I was no longer so close to him and he turned to see what I was doing. I lay back on the bed and barked, 'Did I tell you you could look at me? Turn around, boy!'

He did as he was told immediately. I could see his erection bobbing up and down between his legs. His scrotum was tight beneath it. I enjoyed this sight for a while. He patiently waited for instructions.

'Good,' I said at last. 'Now you can turn to face me. Lie on your back.'

He did so willingly. The light from the cabin window ran over his chest, defining the contour of each muscle with its own sharp shadow. I allowed myself the pleasure of passing my hand over the front of his body, but I took care not to go near his penis.

'Play with yourself,' I ordered. 'Let me see you rubbing that cock of yours.'

He did so. Soon his breath began to disintegrate into short, urgent panting. I slapped his hand away from him. He wasn't going to be allowed to come just yet.

I grabbed the two pillows that had been left for us and pushed them under his buttocks. He seemed to know what I wanted and made no move until he was instructed to do so. I reached for the box, the one Justin had mentioned. In it were rubber sheaths. I took one and, staring straight into his eyes as I did so, I rolled it over my erection.

'Go on,' I said. 'Put your legs up in the air. Show me your fuck-hole. I'm going to put my cock up you very soon. Show me that tight hole.'

'Thank you, sir,' he grunted. He put both his legs in the air, adjusting his behind on the pillows so as to raise his arse up for my inspection. The sight was lovely. This beautiful youth, no longer my master but my servant, his legs raised and his hole ready to be fucked. It was the most vulnerable position I could have put him in. He lay there waiting.

I couldn't hold back any longer. I jabbed my aching cock into his gut. He stifled a cry of protest. I rested inside him for a moment or two, enjoying the feeling of the pulsating muscle around my sex. I leant over his body; our lips were very close. Still he resisted a response. Maybe he knew I was testing him. He slowly raised his arms above his head and clasped his hands together.

'Would you rather see me like this?' he asked. 'Would you not like me tied?'

I looked around quickly for something to bind him with. There was a length of rope holding the curtains in place. I pulled it free and tied his hands together above his head. Keeping my dick inside him, I pulled myself upward to look at him. Very, very slowly, I began to pull back from his arse. He almost yelped.

'Thank you, sir,' he whispered. 'You're my master now. I want to be your slave. Please, sir, please use me. Fuck me.'

He continued to whisper such words as I fucked him. I took my time, savouring the feeling as his arse gripped my cock. He pushed his buttocks towards me each time I went in, straining his wrists against their bonds and breathing slowly and deeply with the pleasure of it.

My orgasm seemed to come rushing up my cock without warning. It erupted slowly, making my whole body tense with excruciating pleasure. As it subsided, I collapsed on top of him and plunged my tongue into his willing mouth.

'I'll be your master, boy. You have what you want.' I stroked his hair. 'My beautiful slave,' I whispered. 'You've found your place in the world at last.'

Ten

The 'crew' (if that's what they could be called, for their organisation was shambolic to say the least) were assembled haphazardly along the deck. There was a general air of anticipation. Dressed in their new clothes, the two strangers were treated like honoured guests.

As soon as they appeared, they were ushered towards two of the four available seats. Opposite was a raised platform. Rock hadn't noticed it when he came aboard the day before. Perhaps he hadn't fully taken in his surroundings, or perhaps it had been built specially for the occasion. What had once been a door was propped up on top of this makeshift stage. It was at something like an eighty-degree angle to the floor: sloping backwards, but not so very far off the vertical. Rope had been nailed to its four corners. Rock immediately guessed what its purpose was to be. He looked around for Justin but he didn't appear to be present. The other men were talking in cheerful voices. Although they used their own language, the tone of their voices was jokey and conversational. They weren't yet discussing the purpose of this assembly.

Dorian was fresh-faced from his bath and looked picturesquely handsome in the coarse trousers and open white blouse he'd been given. His hand grasped Rock's and he waited anxiously to see what would happen. He seemed intimidated by these bluff, cheerful men, even though he now knew they posed no threat to either of them. He was trying to look at ease in their company, but Rock knew him well enough to appreciate his trepidation.

Rock, however, was secretly worried as well. He was concerned how Dorian would react to the spectacle which was about to be performed for their benefit. Regardless of the cruel way Carlos had treated Dorian, Rock thought him to be too gentle a soul to relish watching his own brother suffer what could well be a gruelling punishment. Even with these misgivings, Rock was aware of his dick, stiff and excited at the thought of seeing that sadistic young man endure some of the torture he had so enjoyed meting out to others.

The group of men at the far end of the deck parted to allow a beautiful and regal-looking woman to pass down the centre of the ship. She was dressed in flowing red robes. Her auburn hair cascaded around her thin face like a fabulous waterfall. She was evidently of a superior rank to the men around her. They didn't exactly bow down before her, but they shuffled back and stooped in a half-hearted attempt at playing the courtiers to her queen. She approached Dorian and Rock. Instinctively they both stood and inclined their heads in deference to her apparent pedigree. Her voice was deep and mellow, and every word was given its full weight.

'Welcome aboard, strangers,' she said. 'I am Xania. Please sit. You are our guests here today. I hope you have been looked after so far.'

They muttered an affirmative answer and their thanks. She waved away their gratitude.

'There is no need to feel indebted. I would have done the same for any friend of Justin's. He will be here presently with –' she hesitated briefly and then smiled '– with someone who is known to you, so I believe.'

Dorian coloured slightly. Xania noticed his discomfort and seemed mildly amused even at this.

'Our prisoner is your adoptive brother is he not? He protests his innocence and says you willingly submitted to being stripped and flogged. Would you like to support his story or refute it?'

This was clearly a question aimed at Dorian alone. Rock hoped his friend would not allow his naturally kind nature to overtake his better judgement. After all, Carlos needed to be taught a lesson and Rock wanted to see it happen. Some of his reasons for this may well have been sexual. Rock was not immune to the erotic possibilities of seeing that arrogant devil naked and helpless, twisting his beautiful body in futile attempts to avoid the lash. The image was even more enjoyable for its being morally justifiable. Carlos fully deserved to suffer for his crimes.

Dorian looked at him for advice. Xania stopped Rock's reply.

'No, Dorian. It is for you to answer,' she persisted. 'Do you refute his story? A simple yes or no is all I need by way of reply.'

'Yes,' Dorian said at last. 'He's lying. I refute his story.'

'Do not worry,' she said. 'I am no barbarian. He will be punished, but only for the purpose of giving him a chance to mend his ways. We will not treat him unfairly and his punishment will be only so much as he has earnt by his misdeeds.'

Her cool eyes studied their reaction carefully. Slight amusement continued to play at the corners of her mouth. She wasn't mocking or unkind, just aware of the effect she was having on them and pleased by it.

'You will be given a chance to make plans for yourselves later. First you must see we avenge you as you would wish us to. Your brother is about to be taught a lesson in humility.'

She clapped her hands and Justin appeared, followed by the hapless Carlos. Carlos had been dressed in a loose garment, a kind of gown. It was low down on his shoulder blades and open at the front, revealing his chest down to just above his navel. His hands were tied together in front of him. Justin had hold of the other end of the rope and was pulling him along by it. Carlos staggered forward, his head bowed.

Rock wondered if he knew Dorian and his former slave were present. The supplicant position Carlos had adopted may have been one which he'd been instructed to take, or maybe he just didn't feel able to look his captors in the eye.

Justin, still in his leather jerkin, pulled the prisoner up on to the stage and positioned him facing the door. Two other men joined him on the dais and the three of them soon had Carlos spread-eagled and secured by his wrists and feet to the wood.

Dorian was watching with amazed fascination. He had probably never seen his brother in such a subservient position.

Justin took off his jerkin, revealing the wonderful power of his chest and abdomen. He approached the seated Xania and, to her obvious pleasure, he leant over and kissed her on the lips.

'I'm presuming you want me to do what has to be done?' he asked her.

'It would be most unfair to deny you the privilege,' she returned. 'Unless . . .'

This unspoken question was directed at her two guests. Rock wondered for a moment if Dorian would not enjoy being allowed to scourge his brother's back, but Dorian swallowed hard and shook his head. He still seemed transfixed with the strangeness of it all.

Rock also shook his head. It wasn't that he wouldn't have enjoyed giving the youth a beating he would never forget. He would have loved to do it — if only as repayment for the hurt Carlos had caused, not to him, but to his beloved Dorian. However, he decided to sit back and enjoy the spectacle. Justin was a powerful man; it would be good to watch him exercising those manly biceps and good to see Carlos at the receiving end of his whip.

Justin patted Rock's shoulder. Rock could smell the sweat

which was already building up across his friend's half-naked body. The odour increased his excitement. His cock, unused to being constrained in the material of clothing, pushed against its cotton prison. It did not go unnoticed.

'I haven't forgotten what he did to you,' Justin said. 'You'll have a chance to use his body when I've finished breaking down his impudence a little. I don't want his arse – that's for you to deal with.'

Carlos must have heard this. He raised his eyes and saw the two honoured spectators, presumably for the first time. He was weeping quite openly. Rock wondered whether he had been told what was going to happen to him or whether they preferred to let his imagination run wild.

'Please,' Carlos whimpered. 'Tell them to release me, Dorian. Tell them you always wanted what I gave you. You did, didn't you? Tell them.'

Dorian averted his eyes. Carlos raised his voice to a loud cry.

'Dorian! Please! You can't let this happen to me!'

Justin had joined his prisoner on the platform. The others in the audience gathered round the edges of it, anxious to get a good view. Dorian had his eyes firmly on the floor in front of him. Rock couldn't believe that he really was feeling sorry for his brother. Surely after all they had suffered this could only be seen as proper justice?

Carlos's tears were now falling fast and furious. He was no longer entreating for his release. He must have known there was very little Dorian could do to help him, even if he'd wanted to.

A trickle was beginning to emerge from under the hem of his robe. Carlos was pissing himself.

Justin noticed the warm liquid and stood back a while, waiting for him to stop urinating. When it seemed he had emptied his bladder, Justin reached under the coarse gown and pulled down the prisoner's underwear. It was still dripping with urine. Without squeezing it dry, Justin pushed it into the boy's mouth.

Carlos accepted the gag, knowing full well he would not be allowed to spit it out. Just to be sure he could not, Justin removed his own belt and, with it, secured the dripping, reeking underwear into position. He put his hand in the puddle which had formed at the prisoner's feet and wiped some of the piss across Carlos's face.

This provoked cheers of encouragement from the group of spectators. Justin was triumphant. Carlos represented so much in his life he had hated. The years of slavery which he'd suffered were now to be avenged in this one act of abasement.

The sight of the prisoner, tear-stained, piss-soaked, crucified and utterly degraded, was too much for Rock to just sit and watch without some relief. He reached for Dorian's hand and guided it to his own groin. Retaining his awe-struck expression, Dorian worked his fingers through the material, carefully along the length of the fleshy rod and inside Rock's trousers. Finding the head of the dick with his warm hand, he gently caressed it. Rock spread his legs and sat back in his chair, enjoying the sensation.

If the others noticed this, they didn't seem to mind. They were too intent on what was happening on the platform.

Justin reached for the collar of his victim's robe. He pulled hard and the material began to tear along the single seam which ran down the back of it. Another couple of tugs and the boy's naked back, his buttocks and his legs were exposed. Those watching let out another cheer.

Rock felt Dorian's hand tighten, gripping his cock. He reached across and found Dorian's. His hand slipped easily into the breeches, feeling the wet, slippery end of Dorian's nob. It became hard at once. He began to run his thumb over it. Dorian let out a sigh of contentment.

Justin proceeded to strip the prisoner by ripping the garment from the boy's body. Soon all that was left of the robe was a pile of rags on the floor. The prisoner was naked.

A man leapt up on the stage beside the two of them. He had a bowl in his hands which held oil of some kind. Justin nodded his agreement and the man began to smear this substance over the captive's body. When the skin was glistening and slippery, Justin dismissed the other man.

He went up close to Carlos and whispered something in the lad's ear. Carlos nodded miserably. He was still crying quietly. Justin took a piece of the rags which, only a few moments ago, had covered Carlos's nakedness and used the coarse material to blindfold him.

Carlos began to writhe about in his bonds. It was as if some invisible whip was already caressing his naked body. His buttocks looked especially delectable: brawny and perfectly formed, inviting the abuse which would soon come to them.

The man who had brought the oil now presented Justin with a strap. It was a thick piece of leather, about nine or ten inches long. It was split at the end. The resulting two pieces resembled evil tongues, each with a V shape cut into them. The leather was maybe a quarter of an inch thick. It would hurt the boy, but probably not cut into his flesh.

The first few strikes were surprisingly gentle. Justin merely let the strap contact the flesh, almost caressing it. He started on the lad's arse and then dealt a few heavier blows across his shoulder blades. It was these which made Carlos first vocalise his misery, his protests muffled by the piss-soaked gag.

Before he had time to recover, Justin had whacked his arse hard – three or four times. Carlos tensed his body against the smooth wood which held him down. He was given nine or ten meaningful blows across the buttocks and then the same number across his back. Each strike brought more enthusiastic shouts from the spectators.

Xania seemed to be taking everything in but also appeared to be indifferent to it. Her face was quite impassive and expressionless. It was as though this was something she had often seen. She seemed to take no pleasure in it: merely seeing it done, and done correctly.

Justin soon substituted the strap for a proper whip. He stretched a length of it between his hands and ran this slowly and carefully down the smooth skin of his victim's back. This was evidently to let Carlos know what instrument was about to be used on him. Carlos shivered at its touch.

The lashes came evenly. They varied in their power. Some only kissed his skin, causing it to glow red. Others cut into him much harder, bringing lines across the flesh. All the time this was happening, Dorian and Rock were stroking each other's dicks. Dorian was squeezing tighter by now. He was nearly masturbating Rock fully, but Rock's pleasure was concentrated in the two points where Dorian's fingers touched the sensitive head of his cock. He squirmed almost as much as Carlos but, unlike the prisoner's gyrations, Rock's movements were dictated by ecstatic pleasure. Dorian was gasping slightly as his own member was stimulated wonderfully. He was near to coming.

A particularly heavy blow across Carlos's shoulders brought Dorian's orgasm out of him. He raised himself up in his seat and cried out in unison with his brother's muffled shout. The come spilled over Rock's hand and spread in a damp patch over the crotch of Dorian's trousers. Dorian stayed Rock's hand. Then he returned his attention to Rock's approaching orgasm.

Others in the crowd had openly displayed their dicks and were tossing each other off as they watched the whipping. Rock pulled his trousers down and allowed Dorian to grip him fully with his fist. Dorian pulled at him urgently. It took less than a minute: a great fountain of hot semen spurted over his belly and Dorian's wrist. It happened at exactly the same time as Justin laid down his whip. The punishment was over.

Rock brought Dorian's hand to his lips and Dorian did the same with Rock's. They licked their own fluid from each other's skin. Then they kissed.

Carlos was cut down. He fell on the floor, still blindfold and gagged. Justin leant over and removed the material from his mouth. He put one foot on the boy's head and with it pressed him down on to the other boot. Carlos kissed the leather. Justin pushed still further and, getting the message, Carlos began to lick, his tongue lapping up the dirt. When Justin was satisfied with the one foot, he exchanged it for the other.

Carlos gradually brought his hand down to his groin. His penis was hard and demanding attention. This pleasure was not denied him. After all, to wank himself in front of all those people confirmed that he accepted the judgement which had been passed upon him.

He was instructed to masturbate himself as he licked at Justin's feet. As his orgasm approached he could no longer remain bent over. He knelt back on his haunches, pulling hard at his engorged dick. Justin moved behind him, putting the whip in between his teeth like a horse's bridle. Carlos took in a gulp of air which swelled his upper chest. His stomach tensed and he raised himself slightly from the kneeling position. His head and torso were jerked backward by means of the whip in his mouth – and he came. The creamy substance shot out of his piss–slit, hitting his chest and falling on to his stomach. He gasped for air, shouted some unintelligible words, and then crumpled in front of Justin. He grabbed Justin's ankles and, whimpering what appeared to be thanks, he kissed them, then his thighs, then his legs.

'You're not finished yet,' Justin said. 'Are you ready to be fucked?'

Carlos nodded miserably. He was still blindfold but, nevertheless, his face had an expression somewhere between dejection and lust. Justin summoned two men to help the prisoner to his feet. They stood either side of him, pinioning his arms behind his body. Carlos looked blindly to right and left, wondering where the next assault was going to come from.

Justin approached Rock and Dorian.

'This is your turn,' he said.

It was at that moment Rock fully appreciated how much he had changed. He knew what it was that attracted him to Dorian. He had always known. His kindness was appealing; his looks were definitely exquisite; his body was a joy to behold, but there was something else − something Rock hadn't seen until then. Now he appreciated this and he had a clue to something else. Hitherto, this had been merely subconscious: now he realised it fully. He lusted for Carlos.

Rock had been a slave and therefore denied the chance to express his dominant side. He suddenly realised he had been born to be a master of other men. Although he'd only recently acknowledged it, he had always known Dorian wanted to be subservient. It was this above everything which had drawn Rock towards him and bonded them. It had been so from the very beginning.

He looked at Carlos. He was still whimpering pathetically, but between his legs he was hard as rock. He, like Rock, was finding something new in himself. Maybe all who love in this way must experience both sides of their lust. A master must know what it is to be a slave and vice versa. In the end, one or the other side of the personality will surface if it is allowed.

Rock had seen himself in Carlos's sadistic nature. Even while Carlos was whipping him all that time ago, Rock had known, deep inside himself, that he relished it. He knew what Carlos was getting from it and he wanted that very thing for himself. Carlos's cruelty had been unchecked, unfocused, because he'd been trying to beat his own sense of subservience out of his victims. He'd been only half a person. From now on he would always remember the deck of this ship and his own humiliation. He would be a whole man.

'Later,' Rock heard himself say. 'I'll fuck him later. Take him to my cabin. Let him think over what will happen to him.'

He turned to Dorian. 'It will be amusing to let him stew for a while. Don't you think?'

Dorian was looking at him with undisguised admiration. He was hard again and would, Rock was sure, have taken his brother there and then. It was a measure of Rock's control over him that he pulled his trousers up over his erection and gulped out his agreement to the proposal.

Justin grinned. 'I see you know exactly what you want.

Good. I'll have him sent to you as you ask. Do you want him naked or not?'

Rock considered for a moment.

'No,' he decided. 'Put that piss-soaked underwear back on him. I can't think of a better reminder of his situation than the smell of his own urine. Keep him blindfold and tie his hands behind him. Have his hole greased and make him stand in the centre of the room. Instruct him not to move from where he is placed. Let's see how much he's learnt from his lessons today.'

Justin nodded and went to attend to Rock's wishes. Dorian was about to say something but Rock stopped him by placing a finger to his lips.

'Talking will come later. I'm going to bathe. You will attend to me before washing yourself. Then we'll eat, and then . . .'

He looked over. Carlos had already been tied; now the men were covering his genitals in the yellowing loincloth. He made a vain attempt to struggle and was rewarded with a sound slap across the face.

They led him away.

Dorian took a sponge and squeezed the water from it over Rock's body. He soaped his lover's flesh, enjoying the slippery feeling under his hands. Rock stood quite still with his legs apart to allow access to his balls and in between the cheeks of his arse. Dorian took longer than he needed to in that area, loving the sight of the wet, lathered body hair. When he had finished, he poured clean water over his new master.

Rock's penis was soft now. Dorian risked a reprimand by taking it in his mouth and gently licking the end of it. He wasn't denied this indulgence. Rock hardened slightly and pulled Dorian's head further into his pubis.

Dorian was thinking all the time of Carlos, who would now be standing as instructed, waiting to be fucked. He wondered if he, Dorian, would be allowed to have access to his brother's arsehole. He hoped so.

He had many questions but was content to wait until he would be allowed to ask them.

First and foremost he wanted to ask if he might abandon his previously held rank and continue to serve Rock as a slave. He knew he wouldn't want anything else. This was where he was happy, more so by far than from the fleeting satisfaction he had experienced when Carlos had used him. There was no longer any confusion or guilt: he had always been a slave. Whatever the reasons for it, he knew his own mind at last.

He also knew Carlos would need to revert back to his old self as soon as he was allowed. He had seen his brother wanking himself off after Justin had degraded him. The fact that he had needed to masturbate then, when he was totally humiliated and helpless, had shown everyone that the punishment had not been for nothing. Even so, Dorian realised Carlos was naturally a man who wanted control over others.

Would it be possible to serve both these men? Dorian wondered. Would Rock be willing to share him with Carlos as the two brothers had planned to share Rock himself?

He tried to put his thoughts on hold. Before such a thing could happen, Carlos had to suffer being penetrated, perhaps by both slave and master.

The cock in his mouth was now fully erect again. Dorian began to suck up and down on it. The vague, soapy smell of the skin and the pubic hair mingled with a bitter, salty taste which oozed out of the piss-hole. Rock pushed himself harder and harder into his mouth.

'Take care,' he said. 'I want to save my come for your brother's arsehole. If you steal my spunk, I'll have to beat you until I'm hard again.'

Dorian slowed immediately. He contented himself with gentle, lingering licks around the head of Rock's organ. Rock suddenly stepped back, pulling himself away from Dorian's lips.

'I need to piss,' he grunted. 'Open your mouth.'

Dorian experienced a pang of excitement in the pit of his

stomach. Instinctively, he placed both his hands on his head and, kneeling in the bath water, he bent his head back and opened wide to receive the piss.

A warm trickle hit his face. He closed his eyes. Rock guided his member to Dorian's lips and concentrated.

Then came a spurt of golden, salty liquid. Dorian swallowed it easily. He savoured the hot, strange flavour for a moment before Rock let go and gushed into him.

Dorian swallowed most of the first mouthful of piss: only a few drops of it ran down his chin. Rock paused before letting him have more. When Dorian's mouth was full again, he closed his lips around Rock's dick, gulping down what was there before allowing the flow to fill his mouth once more.

When he'd spent the contents of his bladder, Rock wiped the end of his prick against Dorian's cheek.

'Well done,' he said. 'Now let's see you attend to my arse.'

He turned around. Dorian willingly plunged his face into the inviting crack. He used his tongue to find the entrance to Rock's arse and pushed into it, loving the sting it brought to his taste buds. Every time he withdrew, he lapped around and inside, licking smooth the hairs which surrounded the sphincter.

Rock pushed his behind further and further into his servant's face. Dorian's eager tongue tickled and caressed the shit-hole, the sensation connecting with a yearning glow in the middle of his chest.

But this was only to be a precursor. Rock needed to fuck and Carlos had waited long enough. He pushed Dorian away and stepped out of the water.

'Wash yourself and get dressed quickly,' he told him. 'It's time to attend to Carlos.'

Eleven

Dorian half-expected Carlos to have escaped. The Carlos he knew would never have submitted to being whipped, to having filthy underwear stuffed into his mouth, to being blindfold and taken to await having his arse fucked by a former slave. The old Carlos would have shown his contempt for his captors and, at the earliest opportunity, would have dived into the cold sea and swam, for miles if necessary, until he found land. There he would have gathered together enough support to attack the people who were presumptuous enough to have tried to reform him. He would have taken the disobedient Rock prisoner and he would have forced Dorian to watch while he performed any number and variety of gross acts to compensate himself for the dignity he had lost during his punishment.

So when the two of them entered the cabin to find Carlos there, Dorian felt as though he had woken from sleep only to find his dreams were reality.

Carlos stood, as he had been told to, in the centre of the room. His hands were still tied behind him and he was blindfold as before. He wore the loincloth he had pissed in and nothing else.

His scant covering must have done little to alleviate his discomfort at being otherwise naked. The material clearly outlined his prick: every twitch, every move (and his erection began to manifest itself as soon as he heard the door open) was clearly visible. A pungent smell was given off by the dried, yellow stain over what had once been pure white cloth.

His belly hair, trailing downward from his navel, was tantalisingly inviting as it disappeared into the material just before it spread into the formation of his pubes. The gap in the cloth was loose and revealing around the tops of each of his legs. His bollocks were just visible inside. The sight immediately made Dorian want to place his hand in there and feel the coarse, wiry hair growing thicker and thicker as it vanished from sight.

Carlos had been placed with legs apart in an uncomfortably revealing position. It was clear he had obeyed the order not to move, for if he had, he would surely have eased this strained stance: who would have known? He didn't speak of course, but he did jerk his unseeing eyes towards the sound of the newcomers. He trembled very slightly, but was making some effort to control outward signs of fear. He took a deep breath, sucking in his gorgeous stomach muscles and pushing his shoulders back. His tongue flicked over his lips. He held his head up.

Rock stood in the doorway and regarded the vision for quite a long time. Dorian, just behind him, was aching to satisfy himself again, but he knew his orgasm would be better for having been left until the last possible moment. He ran his hand over the front of his thin, cotton trousers and squeezed the end of his dick gently.

Rock eventually moved into the room properly. He walked around Carlos, admiring the body there on display for him. Dorian looked towards him pleadingly. He didn't yet know what his own role in this was to be. He hoped he wouldn't be relegated simply to being a voyeur.

Rock noticed the look and beckoned Dorian to follow his example. Dorian got close up to the naked body and took his time to admire the muscled tones of Carlos's chest. He took in the sturdy legs with their black mist of hair; the squarely handsome jaw; the wonderful head of thick hair, some of it trapped behind the blindfold, and the broad back, covered as it was in the marks of recent flogging.

Dorian faced the prisoner and slid his hands upward, in between his brother's biceps and torso, pushing further until they reached into his armpits. Dorian had always loved the feeling here: of heat, hair and sweat; the smell it left on your skin; the taste when he made to lick it. He clenched his hands into a fist and pushed into the hollow, grinding against the skin.

Carlos, not knowing who it was or what was to follow, tried to keep his footing and not give in to his evident terror. After a moment or two, he seemed to understand the physical contact was gentle. He let go of his tenseness and even tried to make his armpits more available.

Meanwhile, Rock was attending to his prisoner's back. He traced the spine from top to bottom, pinching gently each side of the vertebrae, massaging gently. When he reached the top of the buttocks, he retraced his path until he touched Carlos's lash-inflamed shoulders. There, too, he carefully dug into the muscle, kneading the flesh and pressing in with his thumbs.

Dorian could tell Carlos was still wary. He must have known he had not been brought here to be the recipient of erotic pleasure. He was here to have his arse fucked. Dorian realised it would be useless to ask Rock to be merciful: he would remain firmly against letting the prisoner go without being hurt.

Dorian put his face to his brother's and began to kiss him. At first he merely brushed across Carlos's mouth with his lips. This contact made Carlos open his own lips slightly. Dorian pressed his body against him, hard and wanting. Their two tongues swirled around each other and their saliva mingled. Carlos visibly relaxed into the sensation. Maybe he knew which of his captors it was that kissed him, or maybe he didn't care. Dorian pressed further and further into the wet, warm comfort of his brother's mouth.

When Dorian pulled back for air, Carlos protested at having this security taken from him. He pushed his chin forward in the direction of the other face. Dorian grabbed the back of his neck and met his lips once more. His free hand trailed over the other's chest and eventually found the nipple. He squeezed and pulled on the teat while his tongue explored Carlos's mouth. His other hand ran urgently through the lad's dense, black hair.

Rock stopped the kneading, sensuous massage and stood facing Carlos's back. He pressed himself into his prisoner. Carlos's bound hands met Rock's penis, which was still covered by his breeches. Rock took advantage of this proximity. He made his lower half available. Soon he was rubbing himself gently in the boy's tight fist. He put his arms right round the other two men and pulled Dorian tighter in towards the centre. The three of them stayed like that for some time, gently rubbing against each other: Dorian and Carlos locked together with their mouths, Rock being masturbated by Carlos's bound hands.

Then, at a sign from Rock, the two captors withdrew. Again Carlos demonstrated his desire for more, but this time was ignored. Rock took Dorian across to the bed and silently indicated he was to strip himself. While he was doing this, Rock, now fully-clothed again, lay back and watched the two of them.

Carlos's penis was straining against its thin covering now. At the head of it, a wet patch had reappeared on the material: pre-come was leaking through. He still stood where he had been told and still attempted to keep his legs apart. Through the baggy gaps in his loincloth, this gave both visual and physical access to the inviting area it covered.

Dorian had stripped only his upper half. He had taken off the canvas shoes with which he'd been provided, and was waiting. He knew it wasn't for him to render himself completely nude. He no longer considered he owned that part of his body himself: it belonged to Rock. His master should be the person to expose Dorian's genitals should he so wish.

Rock turned his attention to Dorian. He beckoned for him to approach. He stroked the flimsy material that covered his nudity, pressing his hand into his lover's groin and pushing with his index finger at the cloth which covered his back-passage.

Then he yanked the trousers down, revealing Dorian's nakedness.

'It's time to use this body that's been left here for us,' he said softly. 'First, I think it would be appropriate if your brother begged for further punishment. I don't like to think we're going to do anything he hasn't craved for.'

Carlos stiffened his body in anticipation. He held his breath.

'Carlos, you can hear where my voice is. Get down on your knees, come over here, and beg to be taken up the arse.'

Instinctively, Carlos reverted to his former, obdurate manner. 'I can't. I won't,' he said.

'That's a pity. You will, of course, but your reluctance to do it at once means we will have to persuade you. Perhaps your flogging was not enough.'

Carlos gritted his teeth. 'Do what you like. Take your revenge. No doubt, in your eyes, I deserve it.'

'Do you deserve it in your own eyes?' Rock asked.

'You are a slave; I am a freeman. No amount of bandits are going to change that fact. What you are doing is wrong and you know it.'

'You think I've been brainwashed, don't you? You think I've lost all self-respect; you think it has been ground out of me during my years of captivity. With your despicable ways, you think you're worth more than me simply because you were born a freeman.'

Rock lowered his voice to give his next words more weight.

'Men are what they are because of what's inside them, not because of the way others treat them. Besides which, you forget: you're not the only freeman here. Your brother is with us.'

'He's not my brother,' Carlos scoffed. 'It's obvious he's the son of some slave. He loves to be abused – he's no freeman.'

'You're making that same mistake again.'

Rock had stood and was stroking Carlos with the flat of his hand. The feeling might well have been pleasant but Carlos presumed it to be the precursor to some hurt and was nervous of the touch.

'Dorian is a slave,' Rock went on. 'That doesn't make him a lesser being. It simply means his natural inclinations tell him to serve, to follow. I was never such a one and, perhaps, neither are you. But one thing my years of slavery have taught me is that you must learn how to obey before you can command.'

He had brought his hand gently up to Carlos's cheek. He stroked the boy's face gently before returning across it with a heavy slap. Despite his earlier mistrust, Carlos was not ready for this. He yelled and staggered backward. Rock reached for the loincloth and ripped it from him. Carlos's heavy, thick meat sprang free. It was still erect.

Rock pushed down on Carlos's shoulders. With his hands tied, Carlos was unable to withstand the pressure and so was forced to take a kneeling position.

Rock beckoned Dorian over. When he was within reach, Rock took hold of his penis and guided it slowly and silently towards Carlos's lips. Carlos took it and began to suck.

While he was doing this, Rock crouched behind him and whispered in his ear.

'You like that, of course. When they made you wank yourself out there, you liked that as well. You liked letting go. Didn't you? You might hate me, or at least you think you do, but you desire me as well. Just the same as you desire this little brother whom you pretend to despise. It's his prick that's in your mouth now, Carlos. You're sucking your brother's dick for him. How does that feel? You're just another cocksucker after all.'

Carlos tried to pull his mouth away but Rock pushed him back on to Dorian's cock, making him gag. Rock's finger traced down Carlos's back and into the crack between his buttocks. Carlos pushed his behind outward. He must have realised straight away that this was not the action of a contemptuous, unwilling prisoner. He tried to remedy his mistake. It was too late. Rock's finger had entered his anus and was exploring inside him.

Dorian pushed into his brother's hot mouth, loving every moment of it. Carlos was not simply obeying orders: he was going further. He was using his tongue to pleasure Dorian. He licked round the head of the thing which invaded his mouth, tantalising the most sensitive parts of it at the tip.

Secretly, he was enjoying this. Perhaps he needed to protest, but he certainly responded to this treatment. His own cock was still stiff and he was making tiny guttural noises in his throat in response to the probing finger up his arse.

Presently Dorian was told to withdraw. He did so, pulling away completely in one movement, leaving Carlos to fall on to his face, his arse still raised. Rock's finger was soon inside him again.

Rock inserted another finger and pushed upward. The warm walls of Carlos's anus were slippery with oil – he had been greased well.

He spoke again.

'Before you are allowed any other sexual pleasure, you will beg me to fuck your arse and then you will beg your brother to do the same. Until you are willing to do that, you will remain here. Your hands will stay bound. You will not be allowed to wank. When you need to piss you will do it over yourself. I will allow you to shit in a pot, but that will be the only concession I am willing to make. Do you understand?'

'I'll beg you for a fucking,' Carlos hissed. 'But I'm damned if I'll beg my brother. You won't make me. I'll stay here and rot.'

'You might be able to go without food and water for a long enough period of time, but your hard-on shows you're not going to be able to resist its needs. You'll do what we ask right enough. When you've done it, you'll be restored to your former self.

'As to your brother – he is willing to remain a slave. I hope that after your experiences you will respect him and all other slaves. I hope you will treat them well.'

'There's one thing you forget, boy,' Carlos snarled. 'You are my slave. I am your master. The only thing you've earnt yourself by this amusing little display is a good flogging. I look forward to administering it.'

Rock smiled. 'You say this and yet you've just told me you're willing to beg me to fuck you. I see that your natural inclinations are too strong for you to resist.'

He lifted Carlos back to the kneeling position. His cock had lost none of its hardness. Rock took it in his hand and stroked it up and down. Carlos whimpered again, unable to carry on his scathing act because of the aching sensation in his loins.

Rock kissed him on the cheek. Carlos turned his face around to meet Rock's and pressed his mouth against the other man's as he had done earlier with his brother. Rock allowed him a hot, passionate kiss, but not for long.

'You stupid man,' he said. 'You're very mixed up, aren't you? Remember this feeling in your cock. You won't get it again until you do as you've been told – until you beg both me and your brother to put our cocks inside your anus. It'll be something for you to remember in years to come. It will be an image which will help you always to keep yourself in check.'

He left Carlos where he was and instructed Dorian to dress once more. Dorian was almost as needful of release as his brother and put on his clothing reluctantly. Rock laughed.

'Don't worry, you'll be able to come soon enough. Look at his cock. It won't be long before he'll beg the entire ship's company to fuck him – if it means he's allowed to let go of his own spunk at the end of it.'

Rock

_____

A man who passed us as we left the cabin was familiar to me.
I dismissed the thought as being unimportant. I'd seen
every member of the ship's company more than once since we
boarded. The feeling of déjà vu persisted, and quite strongly.
Why was this man standing out as someone I ought to
remember?

He was physically like the rest of them. He was not tall, nor
was he particularly short. His body was respectably trim for his
age, which was forty or so. He had a black beard which had
had some attention shown to it. It had been trimmed where,
on the whole, his companions let theirs grow as nature intended
them to. This, and his shoulder-length black hair, was flecked
with grey. He was hirsute, as were nearly all the men on board.
He had very keen, dark-brown eyes and perfect white teeth.
He grinned often (he was grinning now). This gave him a
demonic air which was not unappealing, but somehow inspired
a wish to avoid his company.

I noticed Dorian gave him a look. It could have been a look
of recognition, or maybe it was a response to the look the man
had just cast in his direction. It was clear Dorian was not
attracted to this man.

'Why should I remember him?' I asked.

Dorian moved further away from where the man was now standing. He was looking at the two of us with undisguised lust.

Once out of earshot, Dorian said, 'He seemed very interested in us earlier on. When Carlos was being disciplined, he didn't know whether to look at Carlos's back or our lovemaking. I suppose he's hoping for something from us.'

I looked back over my shoulder. The man was still staring in our direction. When he saw me looking at him he smiled broadly and licked his lips in a lascivious manner. His hand wandered down to his genitals and he squeezed the apparently huge package he had in there.

I don't know what motives I had for doing what I did next. It wasn't as though I didn't trust Dorian implicitly. He had shown me all the devotion and obedience I could possibly have expected from him. Against my better nature, I decided to test him further.

'You are willing to obey me?' I asked.

'Of course I am. You only have to tell me what to do.' He sounded offended by the question. His tone was sincere and I had no reason to doubt it. Despite this, I decided to carry on with the plan which had formed in my mind.

'Wait there,' I told him.

I approached the man. He tried to look coy and appealing. This was a mistake. He was too much the brute for it to work and he succeeded merely in looking ridiculous. I ignored his attempts and challenged him directly.

'You like to watch men rub each other's cocks then?'

He looked puzzled and gave a monosyllabic grunt which I took to be a request to repeat what I had said. I realised he had not understood.

I brought my hand down to my own prick and mimed feeling myself.

'You like?' I repeated.

He obviously understood and, just as obviously, he did like.

I turned to look at Dorian. He was still standing where I'd left him. He looked worried but, when I caught his eye, he tried to remove the expression from his face. It wasn't for him to question my motives, even by showing his reaction to what I did.

'Come here,' I told him.

He joined us. I squeezed his penis through his trousers. It was still almost hard. The man was fascinated.

'You like?' I said again.

He nodded vehemently. I took his hand and placed it on Dorian's cock. 'Feel it,' I said.

Dorian stood impassively while the man squeezed and prodded at his loins.

'If you are to become my slave,' I said to Dorian, 'I want to be sure you'll do whatever I want you to. Even those things you don't find pleasant. It's easy enough to be sucked by your beautiful brother. What would you say if I gave you to this man for an hour?'

Dorian was fighting with his instincts. He wanted to beg me not to. He wanted to ask me why. He wanted to tell me he would hate to be used by this coarse, leering man. I allowed him time to answer.

'It's for you to say, sir,' he said at last.

I pulled Dorian's trousers down and let his cock spring free. The man made a grab for it but I stopped him.

'Dorian, put your prick into his hand,' I said.

Dorian swallowed and slowly moved forward, doing as he had been told. The man grabbed the flesh eagerly and began to wank him enthusiastically. He was muttering something in his own language and his other hand was already pulling out his own huge piece of meat.

I felt strangely detached from this scene. Yes, I was enjoying watching Dorian's strained face as he tried so hard not to let his discomfort show but, more, I was analysing my own feelings of power.

I knew I was not a heartless sadist. There was a long way to go before I would have anything of Carlos's lust for other people's humiliation. Still, the very fact of Dorian finding this act so unpalatable was turning me on. It was much more arousing than it would have been if he were clearly enjoying the experience.

I knew this side of my nature would have to be held in check. I realised it could lead to greater and greater acts of cruelty. Maybe Carlos himself had started with such seemingly unimportant gratifications.

Dorian, trying to be brave, was holding back tears and I knew it. Even this created two different responses in me. I wanted to put a stop to it. I felt that same urge to put my arms around him and tell him everything in the world would be all right: tell him I would always protect him. On the other hand, the sight of his misery, the feelings of sympathy it evoked, were giving me that wonderful golden feeling inside. My cock was hard and my emotions were quivering exquisitely.

I let them boil over and manifest themselves in a good, hard whack across Dorian's backside.

'You're not putting any effort into it, boy. Masturbate into the man's hand. Let me see you give yourself to him.'

He made a half-hearted attempt to speed up his thrusts but he seemed to be hoping I would stop him before he lost himself to the feeling which must by then have been surging up his cock.

I relented. 'Stop!' I said. 'That's enough for now. Turn around.'

The man allowed him to pull away and looked expectantly at me to find out what I had planned next.

I motioned for the sailor to pull his own trousers down fully. His penis was monstrous. It was not the longest I'd seen, but it was long enough and certainly the thickest. Its head was purple and literally dripping: a monster with its own life, bouncing this way and that, ready to bury itself into any dark, warm tunnel.

The sight was too much for Dorian. He took a step backward, shaking his head miserably. The sounds would not emerge from his tense throat. His voice was a hoarse whisper, barely audible.

'No, no. Please, sir, no.'

'I don't understand,' I said, cruelly. 'I thought you wanted to please me. I thought you said it was for me to decide what I did with you.'

The man was now rubbing his cock slowly. He even licked his lips, completing the clichéd image of bestial lust which Dorian found so frightening. He looked from one to the other of us. I was sure he had appraised the situation and was waiting for his cue from me to have his way with Dorian. I took a sheath from my pocket and rolled it over the obscene thing he held in his hand. He seemed curious at this, but didn't protest and didn't remove it once it was on.

Dorian knelt down in front of me.

'Please, master,' he croaked. 'I ask you to remember my love for you. When it was possible for me to do so, I never treated you badly.'

'That's because it wouldn't have suited you,' I returned. 'Do you want me to own you or to love you? Which is it to be?'

'Do I have a choice?'

He said this in a tone which suggested he knew the answer was no. He began to cry, at first quietly, and then he let his emotions go and sobbed freely. He lowered his head to the ground at my feet, his body shaking with the effort of his tears.

I stayed cool. I sensed a metaphorical line in the sand was about to be drawn. I was not immune to Dorian's fear or his misery. I wanted him to go through it and so find out who we were and how we were to relate to each other. I knew that I didn't want our relationship to be based on mere games, on role playing. I needed to know Dorian's desires would complement my own.

'You have a choice,' I said. 'I mean it. But if you decide it's only my love you want there's something you must know. I will give you my love, freely and completely. We will care for each other and yes, we will fuck when we want to, but I will need to find others to command. I need to be a master, a real master. If it's not to be over you, you must share me.'

He stopped weeping and looked up at me. His tear-stained face was beautiful in its sadness. He was wrestling with his conflicting thoughts. I knew he needed to be a slave. It was time he knew what it really meant.

'You will never be just my lover,' he said at last. 'I want you to be my master, but there's something else.'

'Yes?'

'You're everything I've always wanted. I should be happy to serve you and you alone. To serve completely I mean. Even to suck this man, to let him fuck me. I will do it if it gives you pleasure, but . . .'

I nodded for him to continue.

'But, if we are to make these statements here and now, there's something I too have to confess.'

He was trying to find the words to tell me. I wasn't going to help him by telling him I'd already guessed what he was going to say. I stayed where I was, impassive, almost cold towards him.

'It's my brother,' he blurted out at last.

'You mean my prisoner?' I said. 'What of him?'

'He's not made to serve. You know that. He's treated you very badly and he deserves his punishment. But are you going to keep him as your enemy?'

'What would you have him be?'

I could barely hear his next words, they were spoken so quietly, but this was a mark of how honest he was being with himself and with me.

'I want him to be my master as well,' he said.

I turned to the brute who was by now getting impatient. He had stopped handling his swollen organ and was just staring at Dorian, waiting for the boy's arse to be made available to him.

I knelt and put my hand gently round Dorian's neck. We

held each other's eyes for a long time and then I leant forward and kissed him.

'You don't have to go with this man,' I said. 'I only wanted to know that you were willing to. Yes, you will have your brother back and, yes, I will find a way for him to accept me as his equal and you as his slave. Hopefully, he won't be so cruel in the future. I agree your terms.'

We kissed again.

'Get dressed,' I said.

As soon as Dorian began to clothe himself again, the man began to jabber away, protesting at his lost chance. I didn't want to have to admit, even to myself, I had used him for my experiment and had never really intended he should have what he wanted so much. I knew I owed him something.

'Go on to Justin and wait with him for me,' I told Dorian. 'I need to talk to this man.'

Dorian ran away thankfully. The sailor was incensed. I knew how frustrated he must feel and I was responsible for his being in that state. I silenced him by pulling my shirt off and dropping my trousers. I stood naked before him: his prize for being part of my plan.

He had no skill at all. His fucking was painful and mercifully short. As soon as his great weapon was inside me he began to grunt like a contented animal, shoving in and out with no thought to my pleasure or pain. I tried to make my arse available to him, to open it, to relax. It was useless. I was being fucked by a man who might as well have used a hole in the floor.

His loud sigh of relief told me that my ordeal was over. I let him pull out of me. He stood grinning like a little boy who had achieved something splendid for his nanny. He slapped me on the back and stuck his thumb in the air to indicate his satisfaction. Then, without wiping his oozing penis, he pulled his garments back in place and strode off, laughing out loud as he did so.

Twelve

Carlos remained kneeling long after the door had been shut, leaving him alone in the room. The blindfold was secure, as were the ropes which bound his wrists. He could feel the weight of his prick, swollen with his lust. Cool drafts wafted over the exposed flesh of his chest and shoulders.

He felt a dichotomy of emotion. He felt he should be angry. He wanted to feel vengeful. He wanted to assert his superiority over his captors: to himself if no one else. But yet, the darkness in front of his eyes served as a background for a mental image of himself which he found to be irresistibly erotic.

He imagined his own helplessness. He saw his own muscular body, stripped, bound and blindfold. He remembered the flogging he had received and pictured the marks which must now decorate his back. The cool, masterful voice of Rock resounded in his mind. He had been taken prisoner by a man who should be his slave. Now he was to be forced to beg this man and, worse, his own brother, to fuck his arse.

Being fucked was humiliating enough, but to be made to beg for it was almost more than he could bear. He knew he would have to: there was no way out.

He had always known himself to be a master and a cruel one

at that. He took pleasure from seeing others in this position, not from being in it himself. His former superiority had made his fall all the greater. This in turn made his present abject state all the more piquant. From being a person who had always taken a pride in his own body, he had become one who was seeing his abused, naked physique as a sexual thing. He wanted to commune with degradation until he had experienced the very depths of physical ignominy.

Even while he was being whipped he had had an inkling of this desire. He had wanted to beg the man to beat him harder and harder. He had wanted to feel greater and greater pain. He would never forget being forced to wank himself in front of all those people. He would relish the moment when, out of control because of his fear, he had urinated, knowing his own brother was watching.

His obstinacy had stopped him admitting these needs out loud. Before Rock and Dorian had left him, he had behaved as his nature demanded: he had been defiant and proud. His heart, however, had been craving the abasement of his body. He had very nearly given in to his ardour and grovelled at Rock's feet. Now, alone and with this strange desire still unsatisfied, he wished he had done so.

Had he not been bound, he would have reached for his cock and savoured the memories of degradation while he wanked. After he had come, he would have been sated and himself once more. This would have surely given him the strength to resist any further appeals to his latent masochism.

Once he was sure the other two weren't coming back, he edged around the room until he made contact with the leg of one of the beds. He rubbed his swollen dick against it, trying vainly to satisfy his urges. It didn't work. He fell forward on to his stomach and rubbed his front up and down on the floor of the cabin instead. He wanted to come. He soon felt the surge of sweet feeling which meant his spunk was about to shoot from the end of his cock.

The pictures in his mind were piling one on top of another,

fast and furious: Dorian being fucked by the man after the market; Rock, bound to the whipping-post; the gag being inserted in his mouth; he, Carlos, pissing himself and then the feeling of the whip cracking against his back. Above all, a picture of himself as a naked prisoner, blindfold and at the mercy of men who delighted in seeing him suffer for their entertainment.

This last picture was the one that brought his orgasm to the very point of eruption.

He stopped. Some subconscious decision had been made. He wanted more than just a wank against unresponding floor-boards. He wanted what had been threatened. He wanted to experience the most humbling thing he could imagine. He was going to prostrate himself in front of his little brother and beg to be fucked up the arse.

He got to his feet and assumed the position he had earlier: feet apart, chest out, shoulders back. His penis seemed to have a life of its own; the air caressed it and it responded by straining this way and that as though it were looking for relief.

He took a deep breath and, for the first time in years, he felt content and fulfilled. He decided to pass the time until his gaolers returned by thinking about what would happen to him and to what depths of indignity they would force him down.

Rock

————

After leaving the sailor I was able to learn more of what had happened to Justin since he had been sold.

Xania, he informed me, was everything he wanted in a lover. I was curious to know if he was subordinate to her or whether they were equals.

'She likes me to serve her,' he said with a brief smile. 'Although I am far from being her slave. I like being told what to do when we make love. It suits us both. Outside of our sexual activities, we are equals. Perhaps it's like that with you and Dorian?'

'Perhaps,' was all I replied.

I didn't want to define the burgeoning relationship between the two of us. I had a pretty good idea what Dorian wanted from me. There was however, the undisclosed factor of Carlos to consider. I wondered if he would be able to accept me as a fellow master for his brother and, perhaps, for him as well.

I told Justin what I had demanded of Carlos and how we had left him to contemplate his fate. Justin seemed very interested in this.

'Would you be willing to make him do what you ask publicly?' he suggested. 'He created quite a sensation earlier on.

A lot of the crew would like to see him get it up the arse from two handsome men. I know, too, that Xania would like to watch. If that is acceptable to you. Perhaps you'd like to discuss it with your friend?'

Dorian was sitting at my feet. His eyes had never left off gazing into my face. Presumably, he had been listening to what we were saying, but he evidently knew it was not his place to interject in any way. I stroked his hair.

'He will do as I ask. Yes. It will be public. Arrange a place and I'll get the boy. Dorian, you are to go with Justin and wait for us to arrive. You're going to fuck your brother in front of the crew.'

Back in the cabin, Carlos looked much as we had left him. As I entered the room, he fell to his knees. I put my foot to his lips and he kissed it obediently. His lips closed around my toe and he sucked. I pulled my foot from his mouth and pushed his head downward with my heel. He stayed where he had been placed, giving me a tantalising view of his marked back. His shoulder muscles were magnificent, rippling under the skin where his arms were pulled back by his bonds. He must have thought the time for him to be fucked was getting close: he lifted his arse and moved it slightly, anticipating the invasion which had been promised to him.

'Are you ready to be used?' I said. 'Are you willing to beg for it?'

'Please, sir, yes.' His voice was hoarse and low, full of pent-up emotion. 'I beg you to fuck my arse, sir. I beg you, humbly, sir. Please, please fuck me.'

'What about your little brother? Are you willing to beg him?'

He nodded urgently. Clearly he had decided to do whatever was demanded of him.

'It won't happen here,' I told him. 'You're to be fucked in front of everybody. The whole crew will hear you beg for it.'

I lifted him to his feet and felt between his legs. He was fully erect and my touch made him tremble. I turned him round and spread his buttocks, exposing his tight little arsehole. I pushed my finger up him and he tensed. Sweat was running down his back. I probed inside him for a while, feeling the warm lining and enjoying the tightening of the muscle around my finger.

I had with me a small satchel in which Justin had placed a sheath and a length of thin rope. I removed the rope and made Carlos hold the bag between his teeth. I tied the rope round his balls and the base of his prick.

'This is how you are to be led, you piece of filth,' I told him. 'You are to keep to my pace. If you drop the bag or stumble, you will be punished further. Is that clear?'

He nodded eagerly. I was gratified to observe he was as primed as it was possible to be. He wanted this as much as I wanted to give it to him. I tugged gently on the rope. He managed a few steps forward but, confused by his blindfold, he staggered slightly. I used the end of the rope to deliver a few strokes across his behind. They weren't enough to hurt him and he moaned ecstatically, showing he wanted more. I brought the flat of my hand down hard against his buttocks, once, twice, three times. He pushed his backside towards me, anticipating each blow and making guttural noises deep in his throat.

I led him out of the room. Outside, there were several people who had no doubt been told of what was going to happen. They grouped around us, waiting for my permission to handle the prisoner. I nodded and soon they were prodding his body, squeezing at his nipples and manipulating his cock. Carlos stood as still as he was able, but I could see he was on the verge of releasing his spunk. I didn't want that yet. I pulled him away. The men followed us. Although I didn't understand what they said, I gathered they were making appreciative comments about the body on display.

The upper deck was full. Justin had created a space in the centre where there was some sort of trapdoor with iron rings set into it. These were obviously for my convenience. Near to it was the main mast of the ship, which had ropes slung around it. I guessed they too had been put there for our use.

Some of the men were already pulling their trousers open, revealing their hairy, erect cocks. Many were shirtless; some were still fully clothed. There were those among them who did not share their shipmates' lust for their own sex. These, I guessed, were the ones who stood at the back – curious but not involved.

Xania was, as before, seated where she could see the proceedings. Justin was standing behind her, his hand resting on her shoulder. He was stripped to the waist, displaying his lovely, golden flesh. I wondered if this scene he was about to witness would arouse him or whether he was merely expecting a catalyst to provoke Xania into having her way with him afterwards.

I led Carlos into the space. I stood him near the trapdoor and tethered him to one of the iron rings. Then I looked around for Dorian.

He was standing near the front of the crowd, still clothed. He was enjoying the spectacle of his brother being prepared for fucking. He must have wondered how Carlos had come to agree to my terms.

I placed my hands on his shoulders and looked him straight in the eye.

'You are willing to trust me?'

'Yes.'

I gripped him tighter. 'This will not be easy for you, but it's necessary if what you desire is going to come about.'

'Yes, sir.'

I kissed him, pushing my tongue into his willing mouth before ripping his shirt from his body. The cold sea breezes caused his nipples to appear smaller than usual and pointed. The light covering of hair on his arms stood to attention and he shivered. Slowly, I undid the fastenings of his trousers and laid the flaps of cloth aside, revealing the top part of his abdomen and the bush of pubic hair at the base of his hardening cock.

Without letting his penis loose from its fabric covering, I led Dorian to the mast and positioned him with his back against it.

Then I wound the rope around him, securing him to the wood with bonds around his upper chest, his ankles and his thighs. I brought his hands around to the front of him and tied his wrists together.

The two brothers were now facing each other, only a foot or so apart. Carlos was trembling uncontrollably, Dorian patient and willing. There was an eerie silence around us, broken only by the faint noises of the men's breathing and the occasional grunt of satisfaction as they wanked – taking care, I noticed, to stop short of coming.

Removing the bag from his mouth, I made Carlos kneel. I pushed his head into Dorian's pubic hair and held it there for a few seconds. Still denied the use of his eyes, he inhaled the aroma of his brother's groin.

'This is your brother,' I told him. 'Use your tongue to free his cock, but do it slowly. Let me see how good a cocksucker you can be.'

He began at Dorian's belly-button, jabbing his tongue into the indentation and licking around it before trailing down and burying his face in his bother's abdomen.

Dorian strained in his bonds with pleasure. His mouth was slightly open and his tongue flicked across his bottom lip. The movements of his body spurred Carlos on to more urgent exploration.

Using his teeth, Carlos found the flaps of material and pulled them further apart. The base of Dorian's cock became exposed. Carlos closed his mouth on it and gently pulled the organ out of its prison. He sucked greedily, moving rapidly up and down its length, every so often lapping his tongue around the sensitive head.

Dorian began to let out short, painful cries of lust. His bound hands were on top of his brother's head, his fingers pulling at locks of hair. He looked up towards the sky, his eyes wild and wanting. Three of the audience moved forward, getting as close as they could to the two, while still retaining enough space to be separate from them. One of them was completely naked. Of his two companions, one had his penis out, while the other still massaged himself through his breeches. Their hands soon found each other's groins and their lips began to explore the available flesh. This prompted others in the crowd to similar groupings. The beginnings of a mass orgy were under way.

I looked across at Justin. He had pushed his hands down between Xania's breasts and was kissing her neck. She responded with her body to the sensation, but her eyes were fixed on Dorian and Carlos. As I glanced across, she tore her dress from her bosom, letting her tits loose for Justin's mouth. He moved to the front of her. She pushed him down to his knees so he wouldn't block her view. He set about his task with relish. The heterosexual sailors switched their attention to this scene and, like their companions, they began to grope themselves.

I stopped Carlos, pulling him away. He was panting, wanting more of Dorian's cock.

'It's time for you to beg to be invaded,' I said. 'Say what you must clearly, so we all can hear.'

My words caused a hiatus in the frenzied actions around us. Carlos turned to where the sound of my voice told him I stood. When he spoke, it was clear to me he meant all he said. He had accepted his punishment not just because he had no choice, but because he desired it. He needed it.

'Everyone is witness to what I say. I accept you as my master. I, Carlos, am begging you – sir – begging you to take me and to fuck me. It's what I deserve. Please take my arse, sir.'

'And your brother?' I prompted.

'Yes, sir. Dorian –' he searched for the most effective words '– Dorian, little brother, I am sorry for having used you so badly in the past. Now it's your turn to do the same to me. When my master has finished with my arse, I humbly beg you to take me. Please put your cock inside me and fuck me. Use my guts to bring your spunk out of you. When you have done with me, let my master decide what will become of me. I give my body to him and to you.'

Then he bowed his head and let out a great sob of relief. His face was soon running with tears from under his blindfold. They were not tears of sorrow. He was releasing all the hatred and sham which so far had been his armour against his own passivity.

I stripped quickly and sheathed my cock. My prisoner's organ was still tethered to the iron ring. I made him crawl backward on his hands and knees to a point where the binding rope was pulled tight. Roughly and efficiently, I put my arm under his stomach and pulled him up to bring his arse into a convenient position. I pushed his legs apart. His face and shoulders were flat to the deck, his swollen sack and hard dick exposed between his glorious thighs. He laid his face sideways on the hard wood and continued to sob as he was greased again.

I took my time over this. Some of those watching came up closer to get a look at his arsehole. I made certain they were not disappointed. I pulled his cheeks apart and pushed two fingers up him, pulling the opening wide so they could see. He may have accepted his punishment better than I had anticipated, but this did not mean I was obliged to leave him with any dignity. His most private place was exposed to the full. I wanted him to experience this complete mortification.

Then I mounted him.

I slid my throbbing penis into him in one, swift movement. He had no time to adjust before I began to pump in and out. His weeping gave over to gasps. I didn't know whether they were of pleasure or pain, or both.

As the nerves at the end of my cock began to sing, I collapsed my torso over his back. My arms closed tight around the front of his chest as I thrust in and out with short, brutal stabs. I groped his chest and found myself kissing the nape of his neck. He was gasping, 'Yes, yes, yes, sir. Thank you, sir,' as though the words were a mantra. His buttocks slapped against my body forcefully. Quicker and quicker, the rhythm increased in speed until I could contain my seed no longer. For thirty seconds or more I was paralysed by the acute concentration of feeling at the end of my cock. This wondrous sensation ebbed away as my thick, white juice spurted into the sheath.

I made three more forceful thrusts in order to empty myself completely. Then I withdrew.

Carlos remained where he had been placed with his arse still available to me. I leant over and, once again, put my arms around his chest. I pulled him up and further backward so he was kneeling with his chest at an exposed angle. I then took his blindfold off.

After so long in the dark, his eyes needed time to adjust. He blinked several times before taking in the number of people who had gathered to watch his punishment.

His eyes finally rested on his brother. I didn't know whether Carlos had realised that Dorian was also bound. The sight of him tied to the mast, his lovely face wearing an expression of yearning, his penis still wanting more, made Carlos groan with desire.

I took the sheath off my tool and straddled Carlos from the front. I emptied the spunk over the front of his chest. I stepped back and took time to enjoy the sight of it running down him, filling his navel, gathering in his pubic hair. I shoved the sheath next to his nostrils and, obediently, he inhaled deeply, taking in the smell of his own backside mixed with my spunk.

'Breath in again, Carlos,' I told him. 'Remember that smell. It will be on your body for the rest of the day. It's the smell of my come and your arse. Now it's time to add another juice to the filth on your chest. What do you suppose that to be?'

His cock jumped, anticipating this, the most humiliating part of his ordeal. His answer came in a whisper.

'My brother's spunk.'

I slapped his face with one hand and pushed the sheath into his nose with the other.

'They can't hear you,' I snarled. 'Say what you have to say for these gentlemen watching.'

'My brother's spunk,' he cried, turning his head to face different parts of the crowd. 'My little brother's going to come into my arse. I'm going to be fucked by him.'

His gaze came to rest on Dorian.

'Please don't be gentle with me,' he said. 'When you're inside me, remember all the times you've hated me for what I've done to you. Use me as roughly as you please. I deserve to be hurt. Split me apart if you want to, but don't be kind.'

I knew Dorian was capable of giving Carlos as brutal a fucking as he craved: he was certainly ready to shoot his come. He was breathing deeply and slowly. His hands were hovering over his dick. I could tell he desperately wanted to touch his sex. His bonds easily allowed for his hands to reach his erection. Obedient as ever, his will restrained him more successfully than the rope could.

It was time for the assembled company to have a different view of my captive.

I released him from his 'lead'. He was still nervous; I decided to crack him across the buttocks again for no other reason than to see how he would take it. He winced. For a second I thought he might try and avoid a repeat blow, but he checked himself.

He lowered his eyes to the floor at my feet and said, 'Thank you, sir.' Then he pushed his behind outward to make it easier for me to slap him again. I did so and he thanked me once more. It was tempting to carry on spanking him, perhaps to make him bend over my knee. It would have to be done some other time: I was aware of Dorian's need. I had had my turn with this beautiful creature.

I pushed into Carlos's arsehole to see how it had eased after having my dick inside it. I was able to get three fingers up him without any difficulty. I tried a fourth. Carlos was still making every effort to please. He wriggled slightly to accommodate this invasion and gripped the fingers with his inner muscles.

'Good boy,' I murmured. 'You're learning.'

I told him to lie on his back. He did so immediately. I

positioned his body, dragging him a foot or more along the deck by his heels. This must have hurt his back, bringing the marks of his flogging back to stinging effectiveness. He gasped and bit his lip, holding in the cry of pain. I took the rope which had bound his penis and quickly cut it in half. His arms were soon stretched towards the iron rings in the floor and there his wrists were secured.

Some sacking served as a cushion for under the small of his back. I indicated how he was to put his legs: in the air and spread apart. He complied. His bruised hole was thereby displayed as well as if it had been intended for public view.

I released Dorian from the mast, the bindings round his wrists and from the constraints of his trousers (which had gathered around his ankles). I rolled a sheath over his sex and reluctantly withdrew to join the observers.

'Do what you want with him. He's yours. Enjoy him,' I said.

Thirteen

Dorian approached Carlos with slow steps. He knew this was an important moment. After today, Carlos would never be the same person to him.

Curiously, none of the events Dorian had witnessed had diminished Carlos in his esteem. Rather, Carlos had become more of a real person, more human. More vulnerable, yes, but also more the man.

Dorian wanted very badly to come. The sight of Rock fucking the prisoner had stimulated fantasies in Dorian's mind. Although the scene was developing before his eyes and it was real, in his imagination it was superimposed with another. In this, Dorian was the one who was tied to the iron rings and it was he who was about to be screwed. In his mind, Carlos was approaching him while Rock stood over them and watched.

It was not to be. He, Dorian, had been commanded to be the one to fuck and it was for Carlos to be debased once again. The prospect excited Dorian, but it also felt wrong – as though he had been given someone else's clothes to wear or had been forced to adopt a language which wasn't his own.

His brother's hole was there before him, stretched wide by

Rock's recent attentions. His legs, held apart and raised, accentuated its sacrificial vulnerability.

Carlos was looking at him. Their eyes were locked in a steady, calm, gaze. Unvoiced words, unexpressed emotions, were zipping from one boy to the other.

Dorian's impulse was to caress the tortured body before him. He wanted to kiss it and make love to it slowly and beautifully. That love he so often felt which manifested itself in service, in slavery, rose in his breast. It was a love which shied away from being domineering.

Carlos, on the other hand, needed this last degradation. In his heart, he had found a latent respect for his brother. He was grateful for the lessons he'd been taught that day. He'd had to experience the other side of his lustful fantasies. He'd needed to know what Dorian wanted, what it was his own sadism gave to others. Now he knew how good it could feel to abandon yourself to your fate and to the commands of others. He understood why he had so often revelled in seeing others as he was now. His enjoyment of others' lowliness was a reflection of what he felt about himself.

Dorian stood before him now. Carlos wanted that cock inside him badly. The younger boy lowered himself over his brother. His body was straight and rigid: like a man about to do press-ups. Carlos felt the hot flesh of his brother's penis push at the sensitive skin around his sphincter. He bit his bottom lip. He held his breath. This wasn't going to hurt as much as when Rock had thrust into him, but the implications of the act were much greater.

Dorian steadied himself on one hand, using the other to guide his erection into the living tunnel of flesh.

Carlos sighed as Dorian went in. Two young men, brought together as children and forced by fate to be family to each other, now for the first time ever, together as lovers. They kissed and meant it.

Dorian began to pump his dick in and out, slowly and with

great care. He wanted Carlos to feel their union and desire it as much as he did himself. The two kept their eyes locked upon each other. They snatched more kisses, hungry, urgent grabs, each time their faces met.

Around them, similar scenarios were being acted out by groups up and down the ship. Men were sucking each other, fucking, wanking. One young sailor had been stripped and tied to the mast where Dorian had been. He wasn't as hirsute as most of his companions. He was lean and brown skinned with soft, dark hair on his chest and only an attempt at a beard over his chin. His arse was different. There, he had a denser covering of black hair, which diminished just below the base of his spine. His arms were pulled upward above him, bound together and secured to a crossbar. He had been turned to face the mast in order to give three others access to his back. They were flogging him, each in turn, and masturbating at the same time.

Many were still voyeuristically involved with the central couple. These men were grouped very closely around the two and wanking furiously. When one after the other of them climaxed, spunk hit Dorian's back. He didn't care; he didn't really notice.

Carlos whispered to him in between the kisses.

'Go on,' he said. 'Fuck my arse for me. I'm helpless. I'm tied up for you. I'm being forced to take your dick inside me. Fuck me . . .'

Dorian couldn't sustain this pleasure for as long as Rock had. He felt the surge of his orgasm. Before he could stop himself, his semen came gushing up his organ. He grimaced with the rapture of it, shivered, and filled the sheath with his come.

His body went limp. Letting his dick soften inside his brother, he lowered himself full-length over Carlos. Their lips met again. Their prolonged kiss was not an expression of lust, but of love.

Carlos gently lowered his legs. His hands were, of course, still bound. He was unable to hold Dorian, much as he wanted to. Dorian sensed his need but had not been given permission to release the prisoner. Instead, he caressed Carlos, running his hands over his chest, down his sides and eventually finding his ramrod-stiff cock.

He eased himself into a position where he could give Carlos relief. He tried to find Rock to see if this was permissible, but Rock couldn't be seen beyond the group of men around them.

Dorian's hand was already moving gently and slowly, up and down the hard shaft. Carlos could barely contain himself. He writhed about on the floor, trying to dictate the way he was being tossed off.

'Yes, yes,' he cried. 'Let me come. Please! I'll do anything for you if you'll only wank me. You don't have to untie me. Just rub my cock, little brother. Please, please, let me come before my balls explode.'

'I'm not sure if you're to be allowed to come,' Dorian said. 'It's not for me to say.'

Carlos raised his head a few inches off the ground, as much as his bonds would allow. He opened his mouth and pushed his face forward, demanding another kiss. Dorian responded. They sucked passionately at each other's mouths, their saliva mingling and their tongues swirling around together, joined in warm, wet union.

Dorian felt a hand on his back. It was Rock.

'Have you come?'

Dorian nodded.

'Then get off him.'

He reluctantly eased his drooping penis out of Carlos and stood.

'Take the sheath off your prick and empty it over his chest. I promised him that.'

The semen oozed down on to Carlos in great, thick globules. When the sheath was empty, Rock nodded approvingly. Carlos lay there, his expression almost transcendent.

'Do what you must to relieve him.' Rock said. 'We'll mix his own semen with yours and mine. Let's see if he can delay himself coming for more than six seconds.'

Dorian smiled his thanks and, kneeling beside Carlos, he closed his mouth over his cock. He sucked on it long and hard before bringing his hand into play, rubbing under where his lips gripped the hot flesh.

Carlos moaned loudly and pulled on the ropes that held him. Dorian let the meat slip from his mouth and began to wank him instead.

The others around them came very close indeed, no doubt realising the end of the show was close. Those who had not already reached a climax pumped hard in order to come before the prisoner did.

A few came in spurts over him. Others delayed, trying to time their orgasm to coincide with his. By now, he was absolutely covered in human fluid. His body tensed and he gave a little yelp.

'I need your permission to come,' he gasped. 'It's almost there.'

Dorian began to shower him with kisses. His hand didn't stop or slow in speed. Carlos was transported by bliss.

'Let it go,' Dorian whispered. 'Let it go now.'

He did. It thundered out of him. His cries were those of an animal; his release almost more than he could bear.

Others' spunk hit his body from above as the sailors reached their fulfilment. Carlos closed his eyes and eventually lay back. He didn't want to move. He didn't want this experience to end.

'Let's hose him down,' Rock said.

He began to piss over him, the yellow liquid mingling with the semen and eventually washing it away. Some two or three others joined in. Carlos was soon 'cleaned' and ready to be taken back to the cabin.

Once back in the cabin, Rock decided Carlos had been punished enough. He allowed the two boys to climb into one bed. He intended to sleep in the other one, but soon the stirrings of lovemaking reached his ears and he was unable to stay apart from them.

He made Dorian stop what he was doing and pull the beds together as they had been before. He climbed in and soon the three were a mass of limbs, breath, tongues, and cocks. They were now equal and content to express their love and desire for one another.

In the dead of the night, Dorian woke and sensed Carlos to be awake also. He whispered, so as not to wake Rock, who was slumbering gently between them.

'Carlos!'

The hand round his cock, which hitherto he had supposed to belong to Rock, squeezed in response. He reached out into the dark and found the familiar contours of his brother's chest.

'Are you content with this? Is it what you want?'

Carlos squeezed him again. Then he spoke.

'I didn't know I was capable of letting go of my stupid sense of self-importance to that extent. I owe this man a lot. We both do.'

'Don't be embarrassed about what has happened today. I won't ever speak of it.'

Carlos paused before he spoke. 'I want to remember it. I might even want it to happen again. Dorian, you know I'm not a natural slave. I like to be on top. I have to be. But that's why today was so wonderful. I doubt you could ever be as low as I was today, because it's your place to be like that. I set myself higher and, consequently, my disgrace was all the greater. And I gloried in it.'

'I want you to do as you used,' Dorian said. 'I want you to use me. I can't – I can't be the strong one for you. It's wrong for me.'

'I know.' Carlos was now stroking Dorian's semi–erect cock. 'I'll be as I was before, but not so selfish. I don't have to pretend to be unfeeling any more. I've learnt who I really am.'

'And Rock?'

This was still the undecided factor. Rock had accepted Carlos. Would the same be true in reverse?

'He's your master too. He isn't a slave. I see that. When we went to the market to buy him, we decided to own him jointly. That's changed, hasn't it?'

Dorian could feel a warm glow of emotion spreading from his belly upward. It was the beginnings of a fit of weeping, or perhaps laughter, or perhaps love. It was the fulfilment of his dreams.

'It's me, isn't it?' he said. 'I'm the slave and you're both my masters.'

The boat landed the next morning. Xania invited them formally to be her guests.

'You are a remarkable man,' she told Rock. 'I enjoyed the entertainment you gave us yesterday. If you and your two slaves should wish to make your home with us . . .'

Rock expected Carlos to protest. The previous evening, he had told him he was no longer a prisoner and would be afforded the same rights as any other traveller aboard the ship. Xania wasn't to know this, of course. She assumed all was as it had been before.

Carlos didn't speak. He looked towards Rock, accepting him as the most senior person present and expecting him to explain.

Rock put his arm around Carlos's shoulder and hugged him. Dorian knelt at their feet and leant his head affectionately against their legs.

'You see how things are changed?' Rock laughed. 'We are friends now. Dorian will be a good enough slave to satisfy us both.'

Xania, although not impolite, was not really interested in these arrangements.

'Whatever you wish,' she said. 'Will you accept my hospitality? It is your decision. Should you wish to go back to Illyria, or to some other place, I can easily arrange for your transport.'

Carlos flashed a look at Dorian. Dorian mouthed the word 'Father' and Carlos nodded.

'We have to go back before long,' Carlos said to Rock. 'You may not want to return to the place where you were held in slavery, but we have our father to consider. We can't leave him alone with no news of us. Especially . . .' He looked at Dorian again and smiled. 'Especially now he has two sons worthy of the name, not one,' he said.

Rock

A year has passed since the strange events which brought about my new life. Looking back, my old master, Anton, had been fair and just. My situation then had been made easier by the presence of Theo and Justin. I had grown to accept the position fate had forced upon me. I had done my best to keep my true feelings to myself.

Maybe the gods have their own ways of bringing our destiny within our grasp. If this is true and my fate was predestined, then I only wish I had known about it during the time I was held captive.

One other person's story remains untold.

I had not forgotten Theo or the kindnesses he so often showed me. I had once thought myself to be in love with him. I know now that wasn't the case. Rather, I had a deep and lasting bond of friendship with him. It was, I have to admit, tinged by lust. His dark good looks had always melted my heart. I wanted very much to know that he was safe, well and happy.

For those few weeks we spent as guests of Justin and Xania, my wanting to know of his fate was the only thing which blotted an otherwise ideal period.

I was to meet him again, but not for some time.

We were made welcome there. The palatial residence in which the couple lived was comfortable, cool and roomy. Carlos was quite a different person to the one we had known previously. He was no longer afraid to show his gentler side. He was protective of Dorian rather than spiteful. He remained slightly subordinate to me, both in our day-to-day lives and in bed. I presumed this was what he wanted, and I accepted my position as head of this curious group.

Dorian was content to remain subordinate to both of us. Many times during our stay he would be tied to the four posts of the great bed we shared. Carlos would squat over his face, his arse hovering where Dorian's tongue could easily find it. I can see myself in this scene: I am facing Carlos, my arse is filled with Dorian's hard cock. I am fucking myself on it slowly and luxuriously. Carlos is kissing me, moving slowly to allow first his hole, then his sack, to be sucked. I reach between Dorian's spread-eagled legs and find the entrance to his hole. He lifts up to give me better access. My fingers are pushing inside him and he begins to be more insistent with the thrusts of his dick inside me. Soon he begins to moan and I know he is near to coming.

I pull off him and nod at Carlos, who does the same.

'You nearly came didn't you?' I ask. My voice is stern and hard. Dorian is still bucking up and down, unable to relax his body.

Carlos stands over him and Dorian reaches his mouth towards the available cock. Carlos pulls back, just out of his reach.

'Answer your master,' he says. 'Did you nearly come?'

Dorian swallows hard. 'Yes, sir,' he says eventually. 'I'm sorry, sir.'

I look to Carlos. 'Untie him.'

Carlos does so. I already have a wooden chair ready. I decide to let Carlos have the pleasure of punishing Dorian this time. I am going to watch.

Carlos sits on the chair and Dorian stands by the side of it, head bowed, hands at his sides. Carlos has a leather strap. While he speaks, he toys with Dorian's cock. Pulling it, rubbing the head between finger and thumb. Dorian tries not to let this affect his contrite stance.

'Your come doesn't belong to you, Dorian. You know that. You must ask before you let it go. If you come without permission, it's like stealing from your master. You know that, don't you?'

Dorian nods. He wants to be belted; he wants his backside to glow.

'I'm going to punish you now. You're going to be strapped across your arse. What's going to happen?'

'I'm to be strapped across my arse, sir.'

Carlos indicates for him to bend over his knee. When in place, Dorian grips his brother's ankles to steady himself. His arse is in the best of positions for spanking. He can't stop himself kissing Carlos's legs – there so close to his lips.

'Stop that,' Carlos says. 'There'll be time for that when you've had your punishment. Count out the number of strikes you get.'

The belt comes down across the smooth, tender skin. Dorian counts each blow. His voice becomes more and more pained as the beating increases in intensity. After twenty he is finding it difficult to keep up the counting. He needs to vocalise his hurt at the same time. He is given five more. The last two are particularly hard.

He is pushed off his brother's knee. His arse is a warm red. He kneels and kisses Carlos's feet.

'Thank you, sir. Thank you for beating me. Please, sir, please may I be fucked?'

I take him up the arse while Carlos fucks his mouth. With our cocks sunk into the two extreme parts of Dorian's body, we masters make love to each other with our mouths.

At other times we made love together with no hint of dominance or submission. All seemed to be well whatever we did. Even so, we could not stay for ever. Dorian and Carlos mentioned their father occasionally and I knew the time would have to come when we all went back to their home.

This worried me. I was still a slave as far as the older man was concerned. I had no idea how he would take the changes of status which had occurred between us. Dorian assured me he would accept me as a freeman now both he and Carlos did. Still, I was taking a risk by agreeing to go back. I trusted Dorian's view of his father as a fair man who would not make any attempts to put me back in captivity.

The two brothers went ahead of me to explain the situation. I arrived at the house a few hours after them. Carlos was waiting for me. He had been crying.

'What's the matter?' I asked.

'It's all right,' he said. 'I know I look a mess. It's pleasant emotion, not sadness. Father's waiting for you.'

I followed him inside the house. Dorian was the next to greet me. He had a happy smile on his face and I knew all was well. Dorian kissed Carlos and squeezed his hand.

'Father was very pleased to see us,' he told me. 'He thought at first we must have gone back to the island. He sent messages over and received no reply. Then he began to worry. He had seen signs of a disturbance here and feared the worst.'

Carlos took over: 'I walked in ahead of Dorian. Of course, I expected him to be pleased to see me but, secretly, I thought his ultimate joy would be for Dorian.'

He stopped and lowered his voice, still awed by what he had found out.

'He loves me,' he said. 'Not as I always thought – as a second to Dorian. He loves me for myself. He cried and hugged me: he was overjoyed! It's not as though Dorian is secondary in his affections either. He loves both of us equally.'

Dorian beamed at me. 'I told you all would be well,' he said. 'We've explained everything to Father and he's ready and willing to take you into his family as his third son. He doesn't mind what we do together. He sees us all as equal. The only thing that worries him is that we might decide to live elsewhere. I told him . . .'

Evidently, he had been carried away by his enthusiasm. This last bit had been something he had meant to discuss. Instead he had assured his father all three of us would stay here for well into the foreseeable future.

'I can guess what you told him,' I said. 'If it's all right with Carlos and it's clearly all right with you, who am I to say otherwise? We'll live here. I have no wish to go back to Illyria and, pleasant thought it is, I don't want to make my home with Xania's people.'

Dorian hugged me. Carlos put his hand on my shoulder and gulped back more tears. It was still surprising to me that he was more emotional than any of us.

'There's only one thing I want now,' I said. 'I must find out what's happened to Theo.'

I had told Dorian of my need to find my friend. He clasped my hand and hugged me.

'We'll do all we can,' he said.

Fourteen

As Xania had said, there was indeed a register in Illyria which gave the names of those who had bought slaves. It detailed which slaves now belonged to them and where they were to be found.

Rock learnt from this that Theo had been bought by a young gentleman whose name (badly written) appeared to be Barthell.

He went with Carlos to the house where this man was supposed to live but found it to be deserted. A man they met on the road told them Bartell (which was his correct name) had fallen foul of gambling debts and had sold everything. Rock asked if the stranger knew of the fate of the man's slaves, but he was unable to tell them.

'I suppose they were taken in lieu of money. I expect they belong to whoever it was that won the last game he took part in. It could be anyone. The best you can do is ask at the tavern.'

The tavern was not difficult to find. Rock had never been inside such a place before and Carlos had only done so once or twice. The two assumed an air of confidence which was at odds with their inner feelings. They went up to the rough, wooden counter and ordered refreshment.

The warm, flat beer was pleasant enough and the company seemed reasonably affable. Rock and Carlos approached a freeman who were sitting in a corner with a slave squatting by his legs.

The slave was tied to the table with a lead. He was muzzled with a lacework of thin leather straps. A kind of tail, which was attached to the end of a phallus, had been inserted into his arse. His chest was hairy, as were his arms and legs.

His appearance seeming to demand this gesture, Rock patted the slave on the head. The owner laughed and invited the two of them to sit down.

'You like my little dog-slave?' he said. 'I bought him almost exactly a year ago at the market here. He's obedient and very good company.'

'Does he spend all of his time as a dog?' Carlos asked.

'All the time he's with me – yes, certainly he does. Although –' the man beckoned them closer and lowered his voice '– I must admit, there are certain things he's very good at which I wouldn't fancy doing with a real dog. I have a whole kennel at my home. They are allowed to be human only when they are alone together. I make them take turns at coming out on our little walks.' He patted the slave's head as Rock had done. 'We wouldn't want them getting jealous now, would we?'

He reached down and twisted the phallus. The dog-slave reacted to the movement by thrusting his hips forward. His cock jerked to attention. His master chuckled heartily and patted his pet's head again. He undid a strap on the muzzle and held his hand under the boy's mouth. The slave obediently licked his master's palm, trying to do it as a real dog might.

'He'll be getting what he needs later on when I get home. If I don't have too much of this stuff.' He raised his glass which was almost empty. Rock volunteered to buy him another.

'Very kind of you,' he said warmly.

When the drinks had been brought and more pleasantries had been exchanged, Rock asked about the market.

'There was a slave who was sold here last year,' he told the man. 'I'm keen to find out where he went. He was probably given as part-payment for gambling debts.'

He looked at the dog-slave. His hirsute body and dark good looks gave Rock a thought. 'I would imagine he's very much to your sort of taste. He was very like this one in appearance. His owner was a man named Bartell. I don't suppose you know anything of him?'

The man coloured slightly. Rock sensed he knew something, but he shook his head thoughtfully.

'"Bartell,"' he repeated, 'I don't think so.'

He paused for a moment or two, and said at last, 'Of course, if he was given for gambling debts he might very well have changed hands again within an hour or so. You know how people lose at cards. We've all done it.'

He mused on this folly for a moment or two, then added, 'Of course, we've all had our wins as well.'

He seemed to find this amusing. Rock's heart sank. It was indeed a distinct possibility: Theo could be anywhere and with anyone. If the man did know anything, for some reason he wasn't going to say. There was only one hope left.

'We'll come to the market,' Rock told Carlos. 'If he's just been handed around as a stake in a card game, maybe his new owner will want to change him into hard cash. We'll buy him ourselves.'

They left the man and his dog-slave. Had he not been worried about Theo, Rock might well have considered putting Dorian on the end of a leash occasionally. Carlos would certainly approve. Rock contemplated a scenario where the two dogs would be made to fuck each other in front of the drinkers in the tavern.

The market day arrived. Rock found it strange to be able to take in the sights as a free citizen. Even after so long out of slavery, he still half-expected to be apprehended, stripped and put in chains.

He had mixed feelings about going with Carlos and Dorian to view the slaves who were to be sold. He liked the idea of being there as a freeman. He was turned on by the thought of those young men, all naked, each impaled on the phallus-like pegs. He remembered when he had been taken there and thought about the overwhelming feeling of hopelessness.

He also recalled the thrill as he had thought about being sold and who was likely to buy him. Had he known then of the events that would follow, he could have regarded the whole degrading experience as an erotic role-play which would surely have counted among the best he'd ever known.

Maybe Theo would be there now, not knowing that his life was about to be transformed by the arrival of his old comrade.

They fortified themselves with drinks in the tavern before going. The dog man was there again, this time with a different boy. His new pet was also hairy: clearly this was a requisite for the man's predilections. This one had auburn hair and green eyes. Like his predecessor, he crouched, imitating a dog as best he could.

Their friend raised a glass to them. The slave, this one unmuzzled, pulled at his leash and began to lick Rock's leg in greeting. Using his hips, he swished the tail in his arse this way and that. His owner yanked on the lead and brought him to heel.

'Behave yourself,' the master said and gave the slave a whack across the bridge of the nose with the end of the leash. The boy cowered and retreated to his crouched position under the table.

'I don't mind him,' Rock ventured.

The man shook his head. 'You ought to. Look at his prick.'

He put his hand under the slave's buttocks and lifted his rear end to give a backward view of his engorged penis. 'He likes the look of you, that's a fact. Him licking your leg is his way of telling you what he wants – filthy beast.'

Rock looked sympathetically at the slave. His head rested on his hands, while his stomach was flat to the ground. Rock wondered how long they were given to learn these unnatural canine poses.

The boy looked back with large, sad eyes. They might well have been the eyes of a real dog. Underneath their doleful beauty, there was a hint of something else. The boy did fancy Rock and he had more than his doglike way of showing it. Rock felt the pleasurable brush of his own cock against the linen he had taken to wearing as underwear. He was soon semi-hard, his penis trapped by the cloth and held at a downward angle. He tried to adjust his trousers without the man noticing.

'I see,' said their friend. 'He's a fine-looking beast and you wouldn't say no to a bit of a frolic with him. Am I right?'

'No,' Rock answered. 'I don't want him at all.'

Dorian intervened. 'Some other time,' he said. 'We're here for the market.'

Carlos looked at the dog and evidently felt similar lust to Rock. 'I take it your dog is not for sale?'

'Not on your life,' came the answer. 'You can hire him for an hour though. He'd like that. Wouldn't you, boy?'

The slave panted in response. Carlos seemed about to agree. He looked at Rock, who was having the same thoughts.

Rock shook his head, resisting the temptation. There would be other times. His priority that day had to be finding Theo.

The yard was furnished as Carlos remembered it. It was full.

They wandered around. The slaves were priced more expensively than the preceeding year. Carlos took a liking to one muscle-bound young man in his mid-twenties. He had an angelic face and curly blond hair. His skin was almost white and his nipples were soft and pink. His pubic hair had been shaved off and similar attention had been paid to the crack between his buttocks. His cock was circled with a thin loop of string which held a small metal weight. This pulled it downward tantalisingly.

Carlos took the weight in the palm of his hand and then let

it drop. The slave's dick bobbed up and down as the pendulum found its gravity.

'He's lovely,' Carlos commented. 'Look at his eyes. I've never seen eyes so blue. He's really beautiful.'

'He's not Theo,' was all Rock said.

They searched through the rest of the stock but Theo was not there. Rock shrugged sadly.

'Maybe he'll be in the second lot,' Dorian said. 'This is only the very first group.' He squeezed Rock's arm. 'We've got all day. If he's here, we'll find him.'

They were interrupted by the arrival of the dog man. He was smiling as usual, evidently enjoying his day out. Carlos still found his manner suspicious, but he didn't know how to press the matter.

Rock must have been having similar thoughts. 'My friend was hairy,' he ventured. 'He would have made a good dog. You're sure you know nothing about him?'

'You're welcome to come back to my house and have a look at my pets,' the man said. 'It's not very far.'

Rock hesitated. Carlos was keen. Dorian declared he didn't want to go.

'I shan't be offended if you don't all come,' the man went on. 'No doubt you have your eye on one of the boys who are up for sale. You go for him. Your friend here –' he looked at Carlos admiringly '– he can come and have a look on his own. That should satisfy you that I have nothing to hide.'

The 'dogs' were kept in a long, low-roofed building which was one of the outhouses to a comfortable brick dwelling. Carlos followed his host inside. The man's pet was let off his lead. He set off on all fours for an inner room. The two freemen followed.

There were twenty or thirty of them. All seemed well cared for and all were fine specimens of young manhood. They were housed in a straw-covered 'kennel'. Their food and water was in bowls on the floor. Scattered about, there were toys for them to play with: rubber balls, rings, a couple of sticks.

Several of them came to greet their master. They licked at his outstretched hands and butted their heads against his legs. Although only the recent arrival was decorated with a tailed plug up his backside, the others wriggled their behinds in greeting. Theo, however, was not among them.

'I don't put their tails in unless I'm walking them,' explained the man. 'If they want to fuck each other when I'm not here, I don't mind.'

The auburn-haired boy was divested of his tail. He crawled towards a bowl and began to lap at the water in it.

'Do you want to fuck him?' the man asked. 'You can take him now if you wish. I won't ask for payment. I've money enough and you have a slave to buy.'

Carlos readily agreed. He might just as easily have taken any of them: they were all extremely agreeable to look at. He was shown into another, smaller room in which there was a large mattress on the floor. The necessary materials were laid out neatly by the side of it. These included a thick, spiked leather collar attached to a heavy, chain lead.

The boy was brought in at his master's heels. He got up on to the mattress and lay on his back. Suddenly his attitude was human. He spread his legs apart and began to run his hand up and down his stiff prick. He licked his lips enticingly, never taking his eyes off Carlos.

They were left alone. The boy reached over to Carlos and slowly began to undo the buttons on his shirt.

'Are you allowed to talk?' Carlos asked.

'If you want me to,' the boy answered. 'I have to do whatever you want.'

'I'm going to fuck you,' Carlos said. 'Do you want it? Or will you just take it because you have to?'

In answer, the boy brought his mouth to the centre of Carlos's breeches. He began to suck at the thin cotton, tracing the outline of the waiting organ inside. Soon there was a damp patch of spittle across Carlos's groin. He reached down and loosened the fabric, allowing his penis to slap against the slave's face.

The lad continued to lick around the shaft and across the head, pausing to say, 'I want it in me. I did from the moment I saw you.'

'And my friend,' Carlos reminded him. 'You got hard as soon as you saw him as well. Are you sure you wouldn't rather have had him take you up your arse?'

'He reminded me of someone,' the boy said. 'He's very beautiful, but so are you. I am happy it's you who's going to fuck me.'

He reached over and found a sheath. After pulling it over Carlos's sex, he went to a bowl of ointment and smeared a cold, slippery mass over the thin rubber.

'How do you want to take me?' he asked. 'On my back or do you want to fuck me like my master does: on all fours?'

'Neither,' Carlos decided. '*I'm* going to lie on my back and you must straddle my body. I want to relax and watch you fucking yourself while you wank. I'd like to see you come over my chest.'

Suiting action to word, he lay back and allowed the slave to impale himself on the hot shaft. The lad took him slowly inside himself, biting his lip as his arse protested at the intrusion. Carlos used his hands to feel through the boy's chest hair, following the fine lines of rippling muscle. The slave moved faster and faster, bringing intense excitement to Carlos's prick. He held in his breath, making his stomach hard and flat. Carlos placed the boy's hand to his dick, indicating he should wank himself as he was fucked. He didn't need encouragement. He was soon beating his own cock and battering his arse with Carlos's. His body was contorted with effort and sensation. The wonderful stomach, lined down the centre with red–brown hair, heaved in and out. He began to gasp.

'I want to come. I want to let it out on your chest. Please.'

Carlos was close as well.

'Go on! Do it!'

He remembered the fucking he had received on board the ship and thought again of the sheath being emptied over him. He wanted to feel hot, salty fluid running down his naked chest once again. He wanted to imagine it to be Rock's and Dorian's.

They came together, almost in perfect time. The boy shot his load and suddenly relaxed every muscle in his body – spent. Carlos breathed deeply and rubbed the semen into his skin. He raised his torso off the mattress and kissed the slave on the lips. The boy smiled.

'I have to become an animal again,' he said simply.

'Is it all right? Do you hate it?'

'No, I don't hate it. My master's good to us and we're often given to his friends, just as I have been to you today.'

Carlos rose and began to clothe himself. The boy sat on the mattress and watched.

'I hope you'll have me again,' he said. 'I really do.'

'Maybe next time you can have me and my friend together. I don't think he's averse to the idea. By the way, who was it he reminded you of?'

The boy paused, not sure whether he was saying more than he ought.

'I was sold to my present master a year ago. He bought three of us at the same auction. Two of us were happy to have a good home, enough food and a reasonable owner. The other was sad because he'd lost a friend whom he'd been with for some time. His previous owner had been forced to sell them because of lack of money. This slave hated being a dog and, the truth is, he couldn't do it very well. You have to want to or else you keep letting your human ways show through.'

'He looked like my friend? I thought all you dog-slaves were hairy. Rock's smooth.'

'No, *he* didn't. It was the other one – the slave he was so sad to leave – *he* looked like your friend. I was sold in the same batch as the two of them and I saw him being led away to whoever had bought him. He was the double of your Rock –

but he was a slave and Rock is a freeman. They couldn't be the same person. As to the other boy – the slave who came here – he's hairy all right. He's beautiful.'

'His name?' Carlos asked, already hoping more than he dared. 'Was his name Theo?'

The boy looked puzzled. 'We're not allowed names. Why do you ask?'

It was impossible anyway. Carlos was sure Theo hadn't been in the kennel with the other dogs.

'It doesn't matter. Even if he is the person we're looking for he's lost to us. He was sold to a man called Bartell. He must have been given away after some card game.'

The boy smiled.

'I think you might be lucky. Don't for pity's sake tell him who told you this, but my master has a problem with that sort of thing: gambling I mean. He lost everything, changed his name and brought what he could to this place. He wasn't supposed to keep us, but he couldn't bear the thought of us going to bad homes. Now he's made his fortune again he can go about openly, but he still refuses to talk about his past.'

'Do you know what happened to the slave? Who was he given to?' Carlos asked urgently.

'Of course I know what happened to him,' the boy replied. 'He wasn't given to anybody. He's still here, but not with us dogs. He's kept in the house with the servants.'

Rock

I was desolate at the end of that day. Theo was not among the
slaves there to be sold. Nobody appeared to know the
whereabouts of Bartell. I had failed my friend. All my good
fortune seemed suddenly unimportant. Dorian tried and tried
again to convince me that Theo was in a decent home and was,
in all probability, happy and content. It didn't work. I had to
know where he was before my mind would rest.

We were joined by Carlos after about an hour. He'd had his
way with the dog-slave and seemed in high spirits. On his way
back, he'd been to the tavern. He said mysteriously he'd had
some business with the landlord. I confess to feeling angry with
him. He must have known what I was going through and yet
he insisted on being so cheerful. Every time I mentioned Theo
he would just smile and tell me things had a habit of working
out for the best. This, and Dorian's well-meaning but useless
words of comfort, made me irritable and unreasonable.

The man from the tavern turned up again later in the
afternoon. He had yet another slave with him, again on a leash.
I wasn't interested, even though the man seemed very keen I
should fuck his pet – or any other which should take my fancy.

I was suspicious of his generosity. Behind his camaraderie, I detected something else. It was almost a guilty willingness to please. I dismissed this as supposition. Why would such a man have anything to feel guilty about where we were concerned? I tried not to be impolite.

'I really don't feel like I want to indulge myself today. I came here to find my friend. It seems he's been the prize in some card game and I won't ever see him again. You'll have to forgive me.'

'Cards!' Carlos leapt at the word, surprising us all. 'Cards! What a good idea. Let's retire to the tavern and have a game.'

He turned to the dog man who reacted to the proposal by looking distinctly nervous.

'You will have a game, won't you?'

'I don't play,' he said.

'You said earlier that you did. Surely I remember correctly. You said you'd had your losses and your winnings. I'm right, aren't I?'

I protested. This seemed to be a strange way of behaving and I had no wish to partake in a game of cards or even to watch one. Besides, I had no idea how to play. Carlos was determined.

'One game. That's all. We'll play for fun. I tell you what . . .' He took the purse of money we'd brought with us and handed it to the man. I couldn't believe my eyes.

'I'll put up this, the money we were going to buy our slave with. You can put up one of your pets.'

The man shook his head. 'I don't play,' he repeated.

'Or better still,' Carlos went on. 'Any other of your servants that I should wish for. You have lots and, if you lose the game, you'll at least have the satisfaction of knowing they will go to a good home.'

'Who's been talking to you?' the man said quietly. 'Was it that boy you fucked?'

'The boy I fucked? Don't you mean the dog? Dog's don't talk. I assure you he said nothing. He just gave me his lovely little arse. No, he said nothing at all.'

The man had lost his jovial facade. He was angry, or perhaps frightened. There was something more to all this than was at first apparent. Carlos did know something. I decided to back him.

'Surely you can't deny us one game,' I said. 'You can't stand to lose much – just one slave when you have so many.'

The man hesitated and then took the purse.

'I swore I would never do this again. I don't want to but –'

'But you can't resist it,' Carlos completed. 'Come on, I'll let you deal first.'

Dorian seemed appalled at this turn of events. On the way to the tavern, he kept asking me how I could allow it. What did I think I was doing? What if we lost our money?

'Do you think we might?' I asked him.

'Carlos used to play regularly. He's very good, but why do it? Why does he want one of this man's slaves when Father has given us enough money to buy any of the others we want? I know that if we bid we might lose the sale, but at least we won't lose our money.'

Soon we were sitting at a table in the corner of the tavern. I didn't understand the mechanics of the game which followed. Carlos gave nothing away in his facial expression. The man, who by now I was sure was Bartell, seemed to be winning. He sometimes smiled, fleetingly regaining his previous composure. Hand after hand was dealt and the chips piled up on each side of the table.

After half an hour, Carlos had very few of them left. The man held only two cards; Carlos had three.

'I'll go for bust,' he said.

Bartell smiled. 'Are you sure? This will be the end of the game.'

Carlos nodded. He looked worried. I presumed he had all but lost and was making one last, desperate attempt.

Bartell showed his hand: a ten and a queen.

'I've been saving these since the beginning of the game,' Carlos said, his face suddenly triumphant. He laid down a king, queen and jack, all of one suit.

The man leant back in his chair and gave a thin smile.

'Where did you get the cards?' he asked. 'I checked; I couldn't see how you marked them.'

Carlos swept the chips over to his side of the table.

'Surely you don't accuse me of cheating,' he said pleasantly. 'I thought that was more in your line.'

'It was, I confess it. You've found me out, I don't know how.' He gave a resigned sigh. 'Ah well, I suppose this is no more than I deserve. I will be at the market square tonight with your winnings.'

'I have the right to choose which boy I want,' Carlos reminded him.

'I know which one,' the man said. He added sadly, 'He's one of my finest, although no use as a pet. I'll miss him. In return you must keep my secret. I don't want anyone to know who I was before.'

Dorian had been following all this and had, at some point, caught up.

'Bartell,' he said. 'You're Bartell and we've just won Theo.'

The selling had ended and the market square was full of Illyrians and their slaves. I looked around, growing increasingly aroused at what I beheld.

Some of the freemen had the vestiges of clothing about them, but the weather was warm and most had already stripped. Everywhere, captives were being used by their owners.

On the podium where the selling had taken place there was now a large cage. In it were seven or eight youths. Their hands were chained through the bars, their buttocks greased and presented to the outer bars of their prison for whoever might want to take them. As one freeman climaxed into a waiting anus, another took his place.

Men stood in groups, shackled slaves kneeling before them.

These willing captives took into their mouths whatever was given to them. Some were sucking cock, pulling and gagging, trying to get their lips right into the base of the shaft which filled their mouths. Others had their tongues up their masters' holes. Their faces were pressed eagerly into the spread buttocks and their tongues worked steadily – licking and prodding into the fiery openings.

Other young men were being lashed. Some had been made to lie on the floor, some against the walls of the surrounding buildings, and some simply stood unsupported. Belts, whips and canes were being used freely. Cries mixed in with the groans and expletives from dozens of men on the brink of orgasm.

There were also groups who were simply making love together. Some in twos, some in threes or more. They lay on the ground, quietly and seriously enjoying each others' bodies – kissing, fucking, sucking . . .

Carlos and Dorian had told their father of the afternoon's events. Carlos had been admonished, not very severely, for temporarily going back to his old ways and using the landlord's marked cards.

The old man was with us to see Bartell kept to his word. Sure enough, on the stroke of eight o'clock, he arrived.

With him was another. His hands were tied in front of him. He wore a shift of white cotton, open almost down to the waist. His head was covered with a hessian sack.

I knew the shape of his body immediately. Ignoring the people who were with me, I rushed forward and pulled the sack from his head.

Theo stared at me disbelievingly. He brought his bound hands to my face and felt like a blind man over my skin. He was like one who thinks he may be dreaming and needs the confirmation of touch.

Bartell withdrew without a word. I didn't see him go.

Dorian quickly freed Theo from his bonds.

I was weeping; Theo kissed away my tears. On my other

side, Dorian did the same. Carlos and his father faced us, happy smiles on their faces.

My new family closed around me and we joined our bodies in a group embrace.

IDOL NEW BOOKS

Also published:

THE KING'S MEN
Christian Fall

Ned Medcombe, spoilt son of an Oxfordshire landowner, has always remembered his first love: the beautiful, golden-haired Lewis. But seventeenth-century England forbids such a love and Ned is content to indulge his domineering passions with the willing members of the local community, including the submissive parish cleric. Until the Civil War changes his world, and he is forced to pursue his desires as a soldier in Cromwell's army – while his long-lost lover fights as one of the King's men.

ISBN 0 352 33207 7

THE VELVET WEB
Christopher Summerisle

The year is 1889. Daniel McGaw arrives at Calverdale, a centre of academic excellence buried deep in the English countryside. But this is like no other college. As Daniel explores, he discovers secret passages in the grounds and forbidden texts in the library. The young male students, isolated from the outside world, share a darkly bizarre brotherhood based on the most extreme forms of erotic expression. It isn't long before Daniel is initiated into the rites that bind together the youths of Calverdale in a web of desire.

ISBN 0 352 33208 5

CHAINS OF DECEIT
Paul C. Alexander

Journalist Nathan Dexter's life is turned around when he meets a young student called Scott – someone who offers him the relationship for which he's been searching. Then Nathan's best friend goes missing, and Nathan uncovers evidence that he has become the victim of a slavery ring which is rumoured to be operating out of London's leather scene. To rescue their friend and expose the perverted slave trade, Nathan and Scott must go undercover, risking detection and betrayal at every turn.

ISBN 0 352 33206 9

HALL OF MIRRORS
Robert Black

Tom Jarrett operates the Big Wheel at Gamlin's Fair. When young runaway Jason Bradley tries to rob him, events are set in motion which draw the two together in a tangled web of mutual mistrust and growing fascination. Each carries a burden of old guilt and tragic unspoken history; each is running from something. But the fair is a place of magic and mystery where normal rules don't apply, and Jason is soon on a journey of self-discovery, unbridled sexuality and growing love.

ISBN 0 352 33209 3

THE SLAVE TRADE
James Masters

Barely eighteen and innocent of the desires of men, Marc is the sole survivor of a noble British family. When his home village falls to the invading Romans, he is forced to flee for his life. He first finds sanctuary with Karl, a barbarian from far-off Germanica, whose words seem kind but whose eyes conceal a dark and brooding menace. And then they are captured by Gaius, a general in Caesar's all-conquering army, in whose camp they learn the true meaning – and pleasures – of slavery.

ISBN 0 352 33228 X

DARK RIDER
Jack Gordon

While the rulers of a remote Scottish island play bizarre games of sexual dominance with the Argentinian Angelo, his friend Robert – consumed with jealous longing for his coffee-skinned companion – assuages his desires with the willing locals.

ISBN 0 352 33243 3

CONQUISTADOR
Jeff Hunter

It is the dying days of the Aztec empire. Axatan and Quetzel are members of the Stable, servants of the Sun Prince chosen for their bravery and beauty. But it is not just an honour and a duty to join this society, it is also the ultimate sexual achievement. Until the arrival of Juan, a young Spanish conquistador, sets the men of the Stable on an adventure of bondage, lust and deception.

ISBN 0 352 33244 1

WE NEED YOUR HELP . . .

to plan the future of Idol books –

Yours are the only opinions that matter. Idol is a new and exciting venture: the first British series of books devoted to homoerotic fiction for men.

We're going to do our best to provide the sexiest, best-written books you can buy. And we'd like you to help in these early stages. Tell us what you want to read. There's a freepost address for your filled-in questionnaires, so you won't even need to buy a stamp.

THE IDOL QUESTIONNAIRE

SECTION ONE: ABOUT YOU

1.1 Sex *(we presume you are male, but just in case)*
    Are you?
    Male   ☐
    Female   ☐

1.2 Age
    under 21   ☐   21–30   ☐
    31–40   ☐   41–50   ☐
    51–60   ☐   over 60   ☐

1.3 At what age did you leave full-time education?
    still in education   ☐   16 or younger   ☐
    17–19   ☐   20 or older   ☐

1.4 Occupation _____

1.5 Annual household income _____

1.6 We are perfectly happy for you to remain anonymous; but if you would like us to send you a free booklist of Idol books, please insert your name and address

_____

_____

_____

_____

SECTION TWO: ABOUT BUYING IDOL BOOKS

2.1 Where did you get this copy of *To Serve Two Masters*?
    Bought at chain book shop ☐
    Bought at independent book shop ☐
    Bought at supermarket ☐
    Bought at book exchange or used book shop ☐
    I borrowed it/found it ☐
    My partner bought it ☐

2.2 How did you find out about Idol books?
    I saw them in a shop ☐
    I saw them advertised in a magazine ☐
    I read about them in _____
    Other _____

2.3 Please tick the following statements you agree with:
    I would be less embarrassed about buying Idol
    books if the cover pictures were less explicit ☐
    I think that in general the pictures on Idol
    books are about right ☐
    I think Idol cover pictures should be as
    explicit as possible ☐

2.4 Would you read an Idol book in a public place – on a train for instance?
    Yes ☐   No ☐

SECTION THREE: ABOUT THIS IDOL BOOK

3.1 Do you think the sex content in this book is:
    Too much ☐   About right ☐
    Not enough ☐

3.2 Do you think the writing style in this book is:

      Too unreal/escapist ☐   About right ☐

      Too down to earth ☐

3.3 Do you think the story in this book is:

      Too complicated ☐   About right ☐

      Too boring/simple ☐

3.4 Do you think the cover of this book is:

      Too explicit ☐   About right ☐

      Not explicit enough ☐

Here's a space for any other comments:

SECTION FOUR: ABOUT OTHER IDOL BOOKS

4.1 How many Idol books have you read?

4.2 If more than one, which one did you prefer?

_____

4.3 Why?

SECTION FIVE: ABOUT YOUR IDEAL EROTIC NOVEL

We want to publish the books you want to read – so this is your chance to tell us exactly what your ideal erotic novel would be like.

5.1 Using a scale of 1 to 5 (1 = no interest at all, 5 = your ideal), please rate the following possible settings for an erotic novel:

      Roman / Ancient World   ☐

      Medieval / barbarian / sword 'n' sorcery   ☐

      Renaissance / Elizabethan / Restoration   ☐

      Victorian / Edwardian   ☐

      1920s & 1930s   ☐

      Present day   ☐

      Future / Science Fiction   ☐

5.2 Using the same scale of 1 to 5, please rate the following themes you may find in an erotic novel:

Bondage / fetishism ☐
Romantic love ☐
SM / corporal punishment ☐
Bisexuality ☐
Group sex ☐
Watersports ☐
Rent / sex for money ☐

5.3 Using the same scale of 1 to 5, please rate the following styles in which an erotic novel could be written:

Gritty realism, down to earth ☐
Set in real life but ignoring its more unpleasant aspects ☐
Escapist fantasy, but just about believable ☐
Complete escapism, totally unrealistic ☐

5.4 In a book that features power differentials or sexual initiation, would you prefer the writing to be from the viewpoint of the dominant / experienced or submissive / inexperienced characters:

Dominant / Experienced ☐
Submissive / Inexperienced ☐
Both ☐

5.5 We'd like to include characters close to your ideal lover. What characteristics would your ideal lover have? Tick as many as you want:

Dominant	☐	Caring	☐
Slim	☐	Rugged	☐
Extroverted	☐	Romantic	☐
Bisexual	☐	Old	☐
Working Class	☐	Intellectual	☐
Introverted	☐	Professional	☐
Submissive	☐	Pervy	☐
Cruel	☐	Ordinary	☐
Young	☐	Muscular	☐
Naïve	☐		

Anything else? _____

5.6 Is there one particular setting or subject matter that your ideal erotic novel would contain:

_____

5.7 As you'll have seen, we include safe-sex guidelines in every book. However, while our policy is always to show safe sex in stories with contemporary settings, we don't insist on safe-sex practices in stories with historical settings because it would be anachronistic. What, if anything, would you change about this policy?

_____

_____

SECTION SIX: LAST WORDS

6.1 What do you like best about Idol books?

_____

6.2 What do you most dislike about Idol books?

_____

6.3 In what way, if any, would you like to change Idol covers?

_____

6.4 Here's a space for any other comments:

_____

_____

_____

_____

Thanks for completing this questionnaire. Now either tear it out, or photocopy it, then put it in an envelope and send it to:

Idol
FREEPOST
London
W10 5BR

You don't need a stamp if you're in the UK, but you'll need one if you're posting from overseas.